THE SHERIFF'S STUBBORN SECRETIVE BRIDE

MONTANA WESTWARD BRIDES BOOK FOUR

AMELIA ROSE

CONTENTS

This book is dedicated to all of my faithful readers, without whom I would be nothing. I thank you for the support, reviews, love, and friendship you have shown me as we have gone through this journey together. I am truly blessed to have such a wonderful readership.

CHAPTER 1

*S*heriff Josh Ryder sat in his office, his boots up on the desk as he leaned back in a wooden chair. His arms rested behind his head and his Stetson rested forward to cover his face. He was thoroughly relaxed, enjoying the sound of silence. Things had been pretty quiet in Spruce Valley lately, and that's exactly how he liked it.

Josh was the type of sheriff you could always rely on. Just last summer he'd helped his close friend—and often last-minute deputy—Eddie Murtaugh rescue his mail-order-bride, Fiona, when she'd been kidnapped and held hostage after a train robbery. Josh had a strong sense of duty, and what was right and wrong. Furthermore, he always took his position as sheriff very seriously. But every once in a while, it was nice to enjoy a relaxing spring day with just peace and quiet.

After saving Miss Fiona, Josh had received quite a bit of publicity in the papers from coast to coast. At first, he'd liked all the letters he received for a job well done, even though he had to give his close friends credit. He couldn't have done it without his best friend Dr. Sam Slater, or Bright Star, one of the local Crow Tribe Indians. But he had taken the reward money and put it away somewhere safe, intending to do good with it. A part of him wanted to put down roots and build a small home for himself, and perhaps his future family, right outside of town. It would sure beat the small apartment above the sheriff's office he currently occupied. The other half of him liked how things were going for him and he didn't really want to change anything.

Josh never had the opportunity to find female company in the remote frontier town, even after his fame weaved all about Montana. But he didn't want some random woman warming his bed at night. The more he thought of his best friend, Sam, the more he thought about how happy he'd been ever since he met his mail-order-bride, Lucy, almost three years ago now. Josh couldn't help but smirk the first time he'd met Lucy himself. He and Sam had ridden out of town when the stage-coach didn't show up with his intended, and they found her in quite a predicament with a turned over stagecoach.

Thinking about all the men in Spruce Valley that had found happiness with their mail-order-brides made Josh really think about his future. He knew there weren't eligible women in Spruce Valley who were looking for husbands. He'd even considered placing his own mail-order-bride ad in the hopes of meeting someone who could also capture his heart, instead of just being a good-looking woman. He wanted more from a woman than just another body in the house. He really wanted someone with whom he could connect, and thoroughly enjoy waking every morning with.

A knock on the door pulled Josh from his inner thoughts. He pushed back his Stetson and put his feet back on the floor as his chair rocked forward. Josh called for the person to enter just as the handle was turned and the door was pushed open. Dr. Slater's smiling face popped round the door. He spotted Josh rising to his feet, pushing back his honey brown hair. He rolled his eyes, knowing what Josh had been up to all day.

"I like to think that I didn't just catch the good sheriff napping," Sam said as he came into the office, closing the door behind him. Josh chuckled as he shook his head.

"Let's just say it's our little secret," Josh said with a lopsided grin. "What can I do for you, Sam?"

"Care to join me for lunch at The Eatery? It's been a bit slow at the clinic today and I thought a leisurely lunch would do us both some good," Sam suggested.

"I'm surprised you're not taking the girls out to lunch," Josh said. He was referring to his wife, Lucy, her business partner in the women's seamstress shop, Martha and their latest addition, Fiona, who did all sorts of clothing repairs. They had become known as the mail-order-bride trio around town.

Sam sighed in response to Josh's question. "Well, Lucy and I are not seeing eye to eye right now on a certain matter, so I'm just going to let it be for the moment," Sam explained. Josh grabbed his duster off the hook on the wall and gestured towards the door.

"How about you tell me about it over lunch?" Josh suggested. They stepped out of the office together and Josh fished his keys out of his pocket to lock up, before they made their way up the street to The Eatery. Frost's mercantile

3

doubled as many things: in the back was the small café; in the front was all sorts of goods for sale. But it's also where the mail came in on the stagecoach. And ever since Mayor Delphine Stavros had convinced the state to run telegram lines to the small town of Spruce Valley, Frost's was also where Josh had to go to send and receive telegrams.

"I just don't know what to do, Josh," Sam said as they walked together up the boardwalk and across the street to the front of Frost's. "Lucy is obviously pregnant again, but she won't listen to me when I tell her she should really be resting more than working. I'm worried about her health, but she's the independent woman she's ever been." Josh sighed heavily, knowing how stubborn Lucy could be sometimes.

"Must be hard being both her doctor and husband," Josh said, trying to put himself in Sam's shoes. It was one of his best techniques when it came to nabbing bad guys. If he could see the world through their eyes, it was always easier to catch them.

"That's the understatement of the year," Sam said as they entered the mercantile. They said a quick hello to Mr. Frost as he stood behind the counter tending to customers. Together they went back to The Eatery, a small café where Nell was the only waitress there and Emmet and Ella, an older couple, managed the kitchen.

"Good day, Nell," Josh said in greeting as they took to one of the open tables. It was starting to get busy and Josh wanted to place his order before it was too late.

"Hey there, Sheriff. Dr. Slater," Nell said with a kind smile. "What could I get you two today?"

"What's Emmet and Ella cooking today that you think I'd

like?" Sam asked, remembering his wife telling him that Nell liked to be asked instead of told. And just as expected, Nell's face lit up with satisfaction.

"Emmet's cooked up a flaky and delicious Shepard's pie, and Ella's been baking all morning with her cream custard pie," Nell said excitedly.

"Sounds delicious. I'll take one of each," Sam said as he passed Josh his menu.

"Great choice, Doctor. And you, Sheriff?" Nell asked.

"I'll just take my usual, Nell," Josh said as he handed Nell the menu. She jotted down their orders and nodded to the Sheriff before walking away in a hurry. "How on Earth do you get Nell to like you?" Sam chuckled at the question as he watched the waitress disappear into the kitchen.

"Lucy taught me a long time ago that Nell likes to be asked her opinion instead of being told," Sam explained. Josh's eyes grew large as he looked towards the woman. She was in her late thirties, but still moved like she was a young woman.

"I guess that makes sense," Josh reasoned. "She's been waitressing here as long as I can remember and I'm sure that sometimes things can get quite boring."

"That's the secret," Sam said.

"Speaking of, what secret method do you have for convincing Lucy you're serious about her keeping off her feet?" Josh asked. "It can't be easy managing a business and looking after a two-year-old." Sam nodded as he poured them both a glass of water from the pitcher on the table. He took a sip, thinking of his daughter, Francene.

"Thankfully, Fiona has been a big help. She not only

works at the seamstress shop, but she also watches the kids and sometimes comes by to do chores around the ranch house," Sam explained. "But Lucy literally needs to be off her feet. I want her on bed rest, Josh."

Josh ran his fingers through his hair, his way of taking a moment to think seriously about the situation. "Sam, you're just going to need to be stern with Lucy. I know she's a stubborn woman, but this is your wife and child we're talking about," Josh said with all seriousness. Sam looked him straight in the eyes as he nodded.

"And that's why I think you should talk to her for me," Sam said as he leaned back in his chair and crossed his arms. "You have a way of convincing people to do something they don't want to." Josh stared at his friend, not having expected him to say such a thing.

"Though I agree with you, Sam, that convincing bad guys to surrender is one of my skills, we're talking about your wife," Josh said as he pointed to Sam. "*You* need to talk to her."

"But I tried, Josh, and I got no results," Sam pleaded. Josh sighed, always having a soft spot for his friends.

"Fine, Sam. I'll go talk to the woman," Josh relented. A bright smile came onto Sam's face and he couldn't help but smirk to himself.

"Speaking of women, when are you going to get yourself a wife?" Sam asked as their food was delivered to their table. Nell parted with a giggle, having heard Sam's question. Josh scowled at his friend for having been overheard. Spruce Valley was a small town, and the last thing he wanted was to have his business gossiped by everyone in time for dinner.

"I've been thinking about that myself," Josh said once he was sure no one could hear them. He took a few bites of food as he thought of his words. "I'll probably have to post my own ad."

"That's not a bad idea," Sam said as he pointed his fork at Josh. "There is nothing wrong with writing for a mail-order-bride. After all, you know plenty of men who've been successful thus far."

"Don't I know it," Josh said with a shake of his head. "I just hope that if I do start writing to a woman from the East, that she won't be so much trouble as Fiona." Sam chuckled as he returned to his food.

After a few bites he said, "Fiona wasn't trouble. She just stumbled upon trouble."

"You know what I mean, Sam," Josh said. "I just hope that I can post an ad, find a good woman, and settle down."

"Nothing is as easy as it seems," Sam deadpanned. "Just be realistic and open minded."

Josh shrugged his shoulders, unsure of what to say. "I appreciate the advice," Josh managed as they finished up their meal. "Seems I'll go write up this ad and then go have a conversation with your wife."

"Good man, Josh. Always willing to help out around here," Sam said with a grin. He paid for their meal so at least Josh couldn't complain about being treated to a good meal.

As Sam made his way back to the clinic, Josh returned to his office. There, he took out a piece of writing paper and set about writing an ad that he'd have Mr. Frost telegram to the *Matrimony Times* in the East. Thankfully he could trust Mr. Frost to keep a tight lip about his telegram, having sworn before the marshal of Montana to never say a word about what people telegrammed out of Spruce Valley. Not having to worry about the older man telling anyone about his telegram, he only needed to figure out what to write.

What did he want in an ideal wife? He'd always been more interested in a woman's looks that he never thought about what qualities a good wife had. Josh thought about the other mail-order-brides and tried to imagine what had influenced them to write to the men in Spruce Valley. After a while, Josh decided that his ideal wife would have to be thick skinned and able to handle when he needed to go off in the middle of the night to catch a criminal, or help out when asked. His wife would need to be independent and able to look after herself when he wasn't around. With those details in mind, Josh finally drafted his ad. Task completed, Josh made his way back over to the mercantile.

"Here on official business?" Mr. Frost asked as Josh approached the counter with his letter.

"You could say that, Mr. Frost," Josh said as he handed the older man the letter. "I need this message telegrammed out to the newspaper listed on it." Mr. Frost read over the message, and looked back up at Josh with raised eyebrows. First his face read shock, then a wide grin started to spread across his face.

"It would be my pleasure, Sheriff," Mr. Frost said with glee.

"Alright now, Mr. Frost. I hope you won't have loose lips over this matter," Josh said in a stern voice. He didn't take kindly to being mocked, yet he knew that Mr. Frost was a harmless old man.

"Oh no, Sheriff. You never have to worry about that with me," Mr. Frost said as he settled down from his excitement. "But I do hope you'll keep me posted on the progress," he added with a wink. Josh simply chuckled as he shook his head.

"We'll see about that, Mr. Frost," Josh said as he pushed a few coins across the counter to pay for the telegram. "I appreciate you."

"And I you, Sheriff. Have a good day then," Mr. Frost said. He placed the change in the register before disappearing into the back of the store where the telegram machine was housed. Josh turned from the counter and made his way from the mercantile. He looked down the road leading out of town towards the women's seamstress shop on the far side of the road. He sighed as he made his way towards it, wishing he could simply return to his office for a much deserved nap.

CHAPTER 2

*E*mily Middleton laughed as the gentleman across from her said some sort of joke that caused the others in the sitting room to laugh. She was able to follow social cues and began to laugh with the rest of them;, the only thing she was focused on though was the cards in her hands. It was very unladylike to be playing poker with men, but she never turned down a good challenge. Her dear friend Cynthia had invited her to a special luncheon where several eligible gentlemen would be present. And since Cynthia knew how desperate Emily was, she'd invited her as soon as she herself had received an invitation.

As the last card in the river was flipped over, Emily held her breath. She couldn't believe that she'd just gotten a flush. Now all she had to do was keep her cool and hope that her opponents didn't have anything better to beat her. As the final rounds of betting commenced, Mr. Fisher, the man with all the jokes that evening, raised the pot by going all in. The other gentlemen at the table began to fold, obviously defeated. But as it came to Emily's turn to either go all in or fold, she didn't hesitate when she pushed all her chips to the center to be added to the pot.

"Seems like someone's feeling lucky tonight," Mr. Fisher said with a chuckle, another round of laughter circulating through the room. Out of all the women who'd attended as well, Emily had been the only one with enough courage to play with the men. Emily always did enjoy being the center of attention, but she also wasn't going to turn down an opportunity to earn a quick dollar. After all, she had a higher education than most, and a critically thinking mind that often surpassed most of her father's business partners.

"I'm always feeling lucky," Emily replied with a smile as she laid down her cards. Gasps filled the air as they realized she had a flush. All eyes turned to Mr. Fisher as he stared at Emily, his smile quickly disappearing. He flung his cards on the table, showing that he indeed had nothing to beat her. Cheers and applause rose up in the air as Emily smiled victoriously, reaching forward to pull all the chips to herself. With Cynthia's help, the two ladies started to organize the pile.

"Perhaps next time you won't be so lucky," Mr. Fisher remarked as he rose from the table quickly and walked off. He was booed by a few of his friends for showing a lack of good sportsmanship.

"Don't pay him any attention, Miss Middleton. He's just upset that he lost to a woman," Mr. Franklin said to her left. She just smiled kindly at him and stood to her feet.

"I don't plan to, Mr. Franklin," she said. She turned her attention to the others at the table as she declared, "I'm afraid that's all the time I have for today." They all looked very disappointed, especially Mr. Franklin, who had been keen on her all afternoon.

"Won't you join us next week, Miss Middleton?" Mr. Mathews spoke up then. He was a shy man, but his question showed that he'd also taken an interest in her.

"Absolutely, Mr. Mathews. I wouldn't miss this for the world," Emily said sweetly. With her chip tray in hand, she made her way over to the butler who had been acting as banker. His eyes widened as Emily brought her chips over to the older man, Cynthia close behind her.

"How on Earth did you manage to pull that off?" Cynthia asked her in a hushed voice. Her blonde hair hung around her head in ringlets in a way that made Emily wonder why the young lady hadn't married yet. She was a vision in her blue silk gown, yet she knew that Cynthia wasn't willing to marry anyone unless it was for love.

"That was pure luck, my dear," Emily said as she let out a long breath. "For most of the game I had been able to read them pretty good. But that last round was truly just plain luck."

"Why, I can't believe you just won a thousand dollars," Cynthia said as the butler started counting out the notes. "Do you really think that by next week you'll return again?"

"I doubt I'll be accepted anywhere by next week," Emily said as she took the large stack of notes and stuffed them all into her purse. She'd need to return home right away to hide the money. If her father found out she had it, he'd tear her room apart just to take every penny away from her.

"Oh, Emily. It surely can't be as bad as you say," Cynthia

said as she followed her friend out of the room. "You must acquire a husband soon."

"My dear, no one is going to want a penniless woman for a wife once the papers publish that my father just lost everything in a bad business deal," Emily said in a soft voice. She knew that most would still be in the sitting room and she didn't want the dreadful news to run rampant through Atlanta, Georgia before the due time.

"Surely there must be someone here who would love you despite your reputation," Cynthia suggested. Emily stopped her in the hallway then as they made their way to the front door. She turned and addressed her, wanting to put her friend at ease.

"Cynthia, darling, a young lady is nothing but her family's reputation and the friends she has. There is no such thing as true love, I'm afraid. Just good business deals in what we call marriage," Emily said plainly. As she watched her friend's face, she could tell that her words didn't settle well with her.

Cynthia regarded Emily for a moment, having always looked up to the young lady who was taller than her, slimmer with dark black hair and bright blue eyes. She was always the star of every social function, and the type of lady that Cynthia imagined would fall deeply in love with a wealthy man and live happily ever after. It hurt to hear her speak this way now. But after everything she'd had to endure these last few weeks, she didn't blame Emily for becoming so cold-hearted.

"Let's get home before anyone asks about us," Cynthia said as she moved past Emily. They left the manor then, both climbing into Cynthia's carriage. Both their parents thought the other had gone to tea at the other's home, so they needed to return home before anyone became suspicious. With her father now home most of the time, Emily had a harder time getting away from the house. When he'd still been in business, she'd had the freedom to come and go as she pleased since her mother had died in childbirth and her governess was often very lenient, believing women should be more independent.

"What are you going to do, Emily?" Cynthia asked as they approached Emily's house. It was a manor much like the one they'd just left. It was large, historical, and had the most expensive of everything. However, the inside of the house was now rather bare as her father rushed to sell everything he could to keep up appearances. They no longer had friends over and only accepted invitations out. Only Cynthia, her dearest friend, had an idea of what type of hell she was currently living through.

"I don't know, Cynthia, but so far I have a small fortune, should I need it," Emily said proudly.

"Why don't you come to stay with me and my family? I'm sure my parents would understand," Cynthia offered.

Emily shook her head, knowing that would never work. "Once the story hits the papers, no one is going to be very accepting of me, Cynthia. We both know that," Emily said as she looked out the carriage window, the world seeming to pass by as though everything was normal. Like today was just another day.

"We've just been friends for so long that I can't imagine sitting here and watching you suffer," Cynthia said in a pleading voice. Emily looked at her friend then and gave her a reassuring smile.

"Cynthia, no matter what happens, I will be fine," Emily

said. She tried to convince herself of her own words, but sometimes feared one day not being able to live the life she'd always had. Somehow, she needed to find a way to maintain her way of life. She was a Middleton and deserved to live as such.

Thankfully, the carriage had come once more to her house and as the footman came down from the driver's seat to let Emily out, she quickly bid her friend farewell. "Till tomorrow," Emily said as she alighted from the carriage.

"Goodbye, Emily. I'll come pick you up again tomorrow," Cynthia promised. She watched as Emily made her way up the lane to her manor, her pale green gown swishing around her legs. She had a hard time imagining her friend in her current situation and prayed that one day she'd find peace.

Emily stepped into her house and was met by an uneasy silence. The majority of the servants having been dismissed, the sound of the door closing behind her echoed throughout the manor. She hated the sound and detested seeing how bare the house now looked. As she made her way to her room, taking the stairs upwards, her footsteps echoed as well, her walking boots clattering on the wooden stairs.

The moment Emily made it to her room, she closed and locked the door behind her. She took her purse and withdrew all the notes and began to stuff them with the others underneath her mattress. She didn't have to worry about her maid finding her small fortune since her lady-in-waiting had been dismissed as well. All that was left was the housekeeper, and the older woman was no doubt so busy with all the housework that she'd hardly have time to enquire after Emily's needs. Therefore, Emily changed out of her own clothes, finding the action quite foreign since she'd always had someone to dress her. With her father's fortune now gone, Emily had to learn to do much for herself. It was another reminder of how hard Emily would need to work to find her a husband who could give her the life she deserved.

Emily spotted a newspaper on her nightstand as she came to sit on the edge of it. It was one of the last pleasures her father had allowed her to keep. Each day Emily looked forward to reading the paper. Before her father had told her about his sorrowful business dealings that had led to all his money being gone, she'd enjoyed reading the paper to read the latest gossip. But now, Emily feared what she might read, knowing that any day now the news would finally be published all throughout Atlanta. As she read each article, Emily received comfort from not seeing her name in it. And as she reached the last page of the paper, where the *Matrimonial Times* was published, she released a long sigh.

"One more day," Emily said as she started to fold up the paper. But as she did so, a particular ad caught her attention. Emily normally didn't pay the *Matrimonial Times* any attention because she always found the ads uninteresting. She wasn't about to leave her home behind for a penniless rancher or farmer. Emily had no experience in labor work and never wanted to have to experience such a thing in her life. But she saw that this particular ad was written by a sheriff and it caught her interest immediately.

"Surely a sheriff would be able to afford my lifestyle," Emily reasoned as she read the short ad. The sheriff was looking for an independent woman who didn't mind his type of work or the demands of having to leave on short notice.

Emily figured that she was a very independent woman who could take care of a household. And even though Spruce Valley, Montana wasn't a place she was very familiar with, she figured the sheriff had a decent staff. And when she read the end of the ad and realized that this sheriff was none other than the famous Sheriff Josh Ryder, responsible for bringing to justice the train robber gang, Emily's heart thumped with hope.

"This sheriff has to be loaded!" Emily said as she stood and started to pace with the newspaper in her hand. She couldn't imagine why Josh would want a mail-order-bride. He surely could not be in want of any Western woman, so instead wanted someone from the East that had a lot more class. Emily imagined herself being a sheriff's wife, always attending social functions and being an important figure in the community. Emily smiled, seeing herself as that person.

Sitting down at her writing desk, Emily made quick work of writing a response to Josh. She wrote slowly, wanting to show how well her penmanship was. She needed to stand out from all the other letters that he would no doubt receive. She wrote about her family and position in Atlanta, knowing that Josh would be impressed with her connections and the work that her father used to do. Emily didn't write about her current troubles, wanting to appear as sophisticated as possible to Josh. She also made sure to note how responsible and indepen-dent she was, hoping to appeal to every aspect of his ad. And as she started to fold the letter together, she took the only portrait of herself and folded it inside the letter. She hated to let go of one of her prized possessions but knew that she needed to do everything she could to win over this sheriff.

Emily liked the idea of leaving Atlanta behind her and starting fresh in a new place. And the idea of being a sheriff's wife greatly appealed to her.

The moment the letter was ready to be posted, Emily took a few notes from underneath her mattress and made her way back downstairs. She'd have to take the letter herself to the postmaster to see that it would be delivered to Josh as quickly as possible. Emily knew that it would take time for the letter to travel, but in the back of her mind she reminded herself that time was not on her side. She needed a plan, and something quick because she knew that any day now her reputation would be ruined in Georgia. But if she could convince Josh to agree to her coming out to Montana so they could be married, then she wouldn't have to worry about what anyone thought about her in Georgia.

"Emily, my dear. Where are you going now?" Mr. Middleton said as he came out of his study. He'd heard Emily come back after her tea party with her close friend, Cynthia Danny, and was curious why she was going out again.

"Don't worry, Father," Emily said with a bright smile, trying to placate her father. He reeked of booze and the thought of him drinking away any penny he had left made her stomach tighten in knots. "I'm just going to mail a letter."

"Alright, my dear," Mr. Middleton said with a nod of his head. The action caused his headache to increase and he yearned for another tankard. "Just, please be careful." He turned from her then and stumbled back to his study. Emily's smile faded as the study door closed. She turned towards the front door then, determined to save herself from her many misfortunes.

CHAPTER 3

*J*osh's lopsided grin only grew and grew as he walked out of Frost's. In his hand he had a pile of letters in response to his mail-order-bride ad, and even a few telegrams from prospective wives. Josh couldn't believe that his ad had received so much attention, but the more letters he read, the more he realized that his fame for bringing the train robbers to justice had really spread all over the country. His ego surely doubled in size as he read letter after letter that mentioned his triumph. However, that also was a double-edged sword. It seemed to him that women only wanted to write him because he was so famous, and not necessarily because they were looking for a husband. They simply wanted a reason to write someone so brave and daring.

Josh took all his mail back to his office, intent on weeding through all the letters. The first time he'd received a big batch of letters he had made it his intent to reply to each one to at least thank them for writing. But he soon discovered that it would be both a waste of money and time. So instead, he set his mind to discovering which letters would be worth replying to in order to hopefully meet his future wife. Sitting down at his desk, Josh took the time to at least read each letter and sort them between simple letters of praise and letters that related to his ad.

Once the sorting was complete, Josh had a wide grin on his face. He felt good to have received letters in relation to the good work he and his friends were able to complete. Josh was certainly glad that people riding the train didn't have to fear anymore about that gang robbing them. But Josh knew that the point of placing the ad wasn't to attract praise. So, he took all those letters and deposited them in his desk drawer. He didn't just want to throw them away, so for now they'd rest in his desk.

Next, Josh turned his attention to the letters that were written with the intent of marriage. He sifted through all of them, finding that many of the letters weren't very interesting. He sighed, a little frustrated to not have read one letter that detailed a woman he could really picture as his wife. And just when he thought he was done for the day, perhaps needing a stiff drink to settle his frustration, he happened upon a letter that he'd missed amongst all the others. Almost deciding to put it off till he could pour himself a small thimble of whiskey, Josh finally tore open the letter and was surprised when a small photo fell out.

Josh's honey colored eyes grew large as he looked at the young lady's photo. Though black and white, he could tell that she had a long torso, more than likely making her taller than most women. Dark hair flowed down her back in curls and Josh was certain it was black. And as he looked at the young lady's face, he guessed her eyes were blue. Having spent most of his life observing people and their details, memorizing them to perhaps use them later, Josh had a good idea what this young lady would look like in person. He was captivated by her beauty, but as he unfolded her letter, he hoped her words would also interest him.

Dear Josh Ryder,

I'm sure you're called Sheriff all day long, so I figured you could use a break. My name is Emily Middleton and I reside in Atlanta, Georgia. Like most women of leisure my age, my father is a successful businessman that has lent to my years of education and good upbringing. I'm a lady, through and through, but my closest friend, Cynthia, would say that I'm quite a rebel.

Just today I joined a group of like-minded individuals for tea and cards. Most of the women present wouldn't dare play poker with gentlemen, but I'm not like other women. I like to take chances and put my education to the test. I'm pleased to say that I won the final round and took home a very handsome purse. This is not to say I have a gambling addiction, but I do like to push the boundaries on what women can and cannot do.

Society here in Atlanta is very overbearing. I wish to travel West, to seek my own way. But I still understand the benefit of having a husband. Your ad interested me because of what you seek in a wife. I'm strongly independent but enjoy socializing with others. I'm content with the idea of seeing you off in the middle of the night for work because you have a very demanding job. I'd be proud to be your wife and support you in your position in the community. But like Cynthia often reminds me, marriage isn't just a business deal. I would be interested in coming to Spruce Valley to see if we are compatible romantically. Surely, we both desire a family at one point, and marriage wouldn't be enjoyable if we did not like one another.

Since there is nothing holding me to Atlanta because I am now of age, and my father has always been very supportive of my decisions, I would like to come to Spruce Valley as soon as you agree to the arrangement. I know this seems rather sudden, but I tend to act on gut instinct. And my gut is saying that I need to take a chance on you. Either way, I'm overdue for a trip and could think of this as any other vacation. If things don't work out between us, then there is no need to fret.

I hope you approve of the photo I sent with this letter. If you like what you see, reply as soon as possible.

Miss Emily Middleton

JOSH WAS CERTAINLY INTRIGUED by the time he'd finished Emily's letter. She not only had beautiful handwriting, but she wrote with plenty of humor and surprise in her letter that he had to read it a few times before he could truly believe what he was reading. He'd never heard of a woman playing poker before and was surprised she would admit to it. She appeared to be a Georgia socialite, perhaps even a debutante, and would be the last person he'd expect to admit to playing poker with other gentlemen. The fact that she'd won only made him chuckle, thinking she must be a force to be reckoned with.

The only part of her letter that concerned him was her eagerness to come to Spruce Valley. Perhaps she really was bored with Atlanta, or there could be a completely different reason. Either way, Josh had a decision to make. As he looked down at her photo, trying to picture the sound of her voice as he thought about the words she'd used in her letter, he knew that he wanted to take a chance on her probably as much as she wanted to take a chance on him. He liked that she hadn't mentioned his publicity in the papers like all the other women had.

Setting Emily's letter and photo aside, Josh pulled out a fresh sheet of writing paper along with his ink and quill. Then, he set about to writing a response to Emily as he focused on writing as elegantly as she had. Or at least, as legible.

DEAR EMILY,

I certainly appreciated your letter. Thank you for the photo because it really helps to put a face to the author of such a beautifully written letter. I've received countless letters in reply to my ad, but you are the first one to include a photo and to not have mentioned my experience as a sheriff. It's nice that someone can see me for who I really am and not just my position in society.

I will admit that I was surprised that you'd admitted to playing poker. Even here in the West, women wouldn't dare to do such a thing. I can't help but wonder if you'll be trouble for me, but know I write this sentence with a smirk on my face. I am only teasing. I can tell you are a fierce, independent woman. You certainly sound like you'd be able to manage the frequent demands of my position in town. And I think I'd enjoy getting to know the real Emily, too.

Your request to come straight away to Spruce Valley is a little forward, I will admit. But if you truly are only looking for a change of scenery, I'm sure the trip won't hurt. When you arrive, we can take the time to get to know one another with no strings attached. I'd be happy to show you around Spruce Valley, though I'm sure it's nowhere as large as Atlanta. I'm not sure how much you know of the West, but it's very different to the East. As an educated woman, I'm sure you'll take it all as a learning experience when you do take the trip to Montana.

The one thing I can say about Spruce Valley is that everyone here is really friendly. It's a close-knit community and you'll most likely get to meet everyone real quick. We're always eager to make new friends, and there are several other mail-order-brides here that you could get to know as well. In fact, the three of them now run a women's seamstress shop. There are not many shops in Spruce Valley, but we are not without some creature comforts as well.

Really, it's a beautiful place here. Winter has finally passed and the spring air is completely refreshing. Soon, wildflowers will be blooming everywhere. I'd say this is the best time of year to come visit our small little town.

Well, I think that's enough rambling. I look forward to

getting to know you better and perhaps seeing you after a while.

    Josh Ryder

BY THE TIME Josh had finished writing the letter, he knew that it was much longer than what was proper. It would be a pretty penny to mail, and since him and Emily hadn't been officially introduced, his long letter might seem a bit forward. However, he felt very pleased with himself. He liked how it had been constructed and after rereading it, he realized how proud he was of Spruce Valley. Josh knew that it wouldn't compare to Atlanta, but he would be honored to introduce any young lady to this small town in Montana. He couldn't imagine ever living anywhere else and hoped that if Emily did come, that she'd come to love it just as much as he did. He was certain that he could fall in love with a woman as beautiful as Emily, but wouldn't be able to tell till they met in person.

Sealing the letter, Josh took all the other letters and telegrams he'd received that day and put them in the drawer with the others. He'd wait to reply to other letters till he heard back from Emily. He'd also need to have Mr. Frost send a telegram for him to have the *Matrimonial Times* stop his ad. He'd certainly received plenty of responses and didn't need anymore. After all, he was secretly hoping things would work out with Emily because her letter had been so different from the others.

After stopping back into Frost's to mail his letter and send the telegram, he went to the livery stables to collect his horse. Now that he'd replied to a letter, he needed to make a trip out to the Slater Ranch. After talking to Lucy about her needing to rest in bed till she was no longer expecting, she'd in turn struck a deal with him. He needed to keep her up to date on all the happenings in town and also tell her that he'd finally written to a young lady. Always a man who kept his promises, Josh lead his mare out of town towards the ranch to deliver the news to Mrs. Slater.

CHAPTER 4

*E*mily paced in the sitting room, feeling her heart pounding in her chest. She had dressed herself in a simple day gown, knowing that she wouldn't be entertaining anyone for a long time. That morning, the papers had finally printed the horrible story surrounding her father. She hadn't seen her father so far that day, but was certain he would know what had transpired already.

Emily was certain what she should do now. With her reputation being tarnished, she didn't dare call on any of her acquaintances. She understood how debutantes acted towards those who had lost everything. She herself had done it before and was certain that this was some type of karmic revenge for the way she'd treated others in the past. She let out a deep sigh, doing her best to settle her nerves. She didn't want to cry but could feel tears pooling in the corner of her eyes.

A knock on the sitting room door startled her, causing her to cry out in fright. She was so on edge that any little thing seemed to unnerve her. Gathering her courage, she called for the knocker to come in. She let out a sigh of relief as Cynthia opened the door and came strolling in.

"Oh, Emily. I came as soon as I could," Cynthia said as she wrapped her arms around her dearest friend. "I'm sure my parents won't be pleased and would scold me for risking being seen with you. But frankly, my dear, I don't give a damn."

Emily chuckled as she held her friend closely. "You never cease to surprise me, Cynthia," Emily said as she stepped back from her friend. "You were once so quiet and shy, and now you are almost as rebellious as I am."

"Why thank you," Cynthia said with a proud smile. They then sat down together on the couch, one of the last few remaining pieces of furniture in the room. "So, how are you doing?"

Emily shook her head as she said, "I simply don't know what I'm going to do."

"Have you heard back from the sheriff you wrote to?" Cynthia asked, trying to remain hopeful for her dear friend.

"I have not. But just in case, I'm packed for the trip. I decided to only pack one trunk. I figured I can order more gowns once I reach Spruce Valley and have become engaged to the sheriff," Emily explained.

"I can't imagine traveling with one trunk," Cynthia said, concerned. "Why don't you let me pay for another trunk to go with you? Surely you still have gowns and things to fill it?"

"I have plenty, Cynthia, but I must think of what I can carry alone," Emily said, always being reasonable. "The train to Montana is almost two weeks long, with a few days by stagecoach to reach Spruce Valley thereafter. I don't want to travel with too many things." Cynthia shook her head, having a hard time imaging traveling for that long alone.

"I wish you had someone to go with you," Cynthia said. "I hate the idea of you being on your own."

Emily gave Cynthia a wicked grin as she said, "Then why don't you come with me? We could both find wealthy husbands in the West." Cynthia laughed then as she shook her head, a sound Emily found pleasing to the ear. It was good to know that at least she could make her friend laugh.

"I'm not as brave as you, Emily," Cynthia admitted. "I might one day gather the courage to play a hand of poker with the men, but I could never leave my family behind."

"I don't blame you, Cynthia. You have a great family," Emily said. "And I'm sure that if my mother had survived childbirth, none of this would have happened." The two sighed together as their eyes drifted around the bare room. Once, the room had held many prized possessions and Emily had always been proud anytime they'd have company over. She always thought this manor was the most elegant of any in Atlanta. Now it was just a shell of a ghost of what once was.

"Excuse me, Miss Middleton," Mrs. Silver, the house-keeper, said as she came into the sitting room. "The mail has just come in." The housekeeper handed the mail over to Emily before turning and quickly leaving. The front door opened and closed then, telling the young ladies that Mrs. Silver had left the house for the last time. Emily knew that she was truly on her own then and couldn't even rely on her father for anything.

"Well, hurry up and see what has come," Cynthia encouraged, pulling Emily from her thoughts. Emily gave her friend a kind smile as she started flipping through the letters. Most were addressed to her father, having been sent out that morning. She could only assume that they were sent with anger and hate, so she set them aside with the intent of perhaps never showing her father. But she did find one addressed to herself. As she flipped it over and saw that it was from Spruce Valley, hope leapt into her heart.

"My goodness, he's written me!" Emily said excitedly as she tore open the letter and read it as quickly as she could. "And he's agreed to my coming to Spruce Valley!" The ladies cheered together as relief flooded Emily. At least now she had some place to go.

"How does he feel about what has happened to your father?" Cynthia asked, eager to read the letter herself. But Emily quickly folded it back up.

"I haven't told him yet," Emily admitted. "I will go to Spruce Valley and see how I like it before I confess everything to him." Cynthia was stunned into silence by her friend's words. She didn't dare believe that Emily had deceived the sheriff.

"Then what on Earth did you tell the man?" Cynthia asked, perplexed.

"I simply wrote that I desired a change of scenery and that Spruce Valley would make for a good vacation," Emily explained, unable to meet her friend's stare. "I wrote that if things didn't work out, then there would be no hard feelings."

"Oh, Emily. But what if things do work out and he proposes? Then you're going to have to tell him the truth of everything and perhaps the truth will hurt too much," Cynthia said, more concerned than ever.

"What does that matter?" Emily said as she looked up

finally. "It's not like the sheriff would be marrying me for my money. He no doubt finds me beautiful enough to have for a wife, for I sent my photo with my letter."

"My dear, there is more to marriage than the union of two attractive people," Cynthia said with a sigh. "He'll want to know your true character."

"I have been honest about other things and will do my best to remain honest about my expectations of marriage," Emily said as she stood. "But I must go acquire a train ticket now."

"Emily, don't be cross with me. We shall never see each other again after this," Cynthia said. Emily stopped dead in her tracks, Cynthia's words settling over her. She knew her friend was right and that she shouldn't just turn her back on her.

Emily turned to her friend, a deep frown on her face. "I'm so sorry, Cynthia. I know you are only looking out for me," Emily said as she returned to her friend and embraced her. "I shall surely miss you the most."

"And I, you," Cynthia replied as she held her friend close. She tried not to cry but could feel the tears trickling down her face.

"Now, about this ticket," Cynthia said as she pulled away from her friend and quickly wiped her eyes on her handkerchief. "I shall go down to the station and purchase it for you, and don't you dare try to stop me." Cynthia raised a finger at Emily as she tried to speak up against the idea.

"You should not show yourself in public but instead, slip away in the night. It's the only way to preserve one's image in Atlanta, should you need to return," Cynthia explained. "There shall be so much mystery about your disappearance that there shall be rumors about you for years to come." Both young ladies smiled and laughed about the idea as they embraced once more.

"Fine then. I shall see you off and look forward to your return," Emily said as she walked Cynthia to the front door.

"And I shall make sure to return with some food as well," Cynthia said, looking about the empty house. "I'm not sure what you have left."

"I'm sure I can put something together in the kitchen," Emily said as she tried to reassure her.

"I hope this sheriff staffs a good household," Cynthia said with a sigh. "You truly do deserve the best in the world."

"I hope the same," Emily said as she pulled open the door for Cynthia. It was an action so below her station that she shivered for a moment, thinking how low she'd come from a debutante to someone opening her own door.

"Alright then, I shall be back after a while," Cynthia said with a dark expression on her face. She left the house quickly and hurried down the stairs to her waiting carriage. Emily didn't wait to see her off but instead quickly shut the door, as though people might be lurking around to catch a glimpse of the most sought after debutante in Atlanta who had just fallen as low as you could in this city.

Left alone, Emily finally let the tears that she'd held back all morning fall. She walked towards the kitchen with the sheriff's letter still in her hand. She was thankful that the man was willing to take a chance on her and would hopefully continue to support her way of life, once she reached Spruce Valley. She had a large sum of money to travel with and had done well to sew it into the sides of her trunk, in case it would ever be searched. Emily knew that she would have a little to live on until things could be made official between her and Josh, but she only hoped that their courtship and engagement would be short.

Emily did her best to get her emotions under wraps as she made her way to the kitchen. There, she rummaged around in the pantry till she found some bread, jam, butter and cheese. Emily had never prepared her own food before and found the action rather odd. But, she needed to eat something and this was all that she could find. Sitting down on a stool at the center counter of the kitchen, she ate the food quietly, listening to the silence of the empty house. Emily knew that her hours left in the manor were numbered, and she eagerly looked forward to Cynthia's return. By midnight, she hoped to be on a train headed West.

CHAPTER 5

The back and forth rocking of the train put Emily's nerves on edge. She didn't like the movement of the train and often fought it, finding herself being slightly tasseled back and forth. Emily was at least thankful that Cynthia had paid for her to have her own private room on the train, but often couldn't find a very comfortable position to sit or sleep on the metal beast.

When she'd left Atlanta in the middle of the night, she'd been excited to leave her old life behind her. She was setting off for the West like many before her, to seek a better life for herself. She was going to meet a famous sheriff whom she was convinced she could seduce into marrying her. Then, she'd have every comfort in life she'd been used to and plenty of social outings with her new husband to enjoy. Emily only had to endure getting to Spruce Valley first.

The first few days of the train ride had been spent staying

put in her room. She'd sometimes stare out of the window, eager to see the scenery change. She couldn't wait to see what the West looked like, but for the most part the train's views were of only cluttered forests, broken up by various small towns. Nothing reminded her of Atlanta, and since this was her first time traveling outside the city, she was a bit nervous to see nothing familiar.

After she'd gotten used to the flow of the train, she started to venture out of her room in hopes of socializing with other people. Emily was so used to being the center of attention that she'd started to crave some sort of conversation with another person. Eventually she got over her fear that someone on the train might know her and her reputation in Atlanta. She started taking the time to walk the train, sitting in the public carriages, and sometimes striking up conversation with other ladies traveling. But every time they found out that she was traveling alone without a chaperone, their conversations often stopped. Even when Emily mentioned she was traveling West to be a mail-order-bride to the famous Sheriff Josh Ryder, it didn't give her any leeway. Emily was quickly learning that people in the West valued other things that Emily always thought everyone cherished above others. She now understood the weight and importance for a woman to have a husband more than anything, which Emily found very overwhelming.

Not only was the company poor while traveling by train, but also the food. She dined in the dining cart for every meal since she had the extra cash to do so, but the same old food over and over again started to become very boring. She even thought of getting off the train at the many stops in various towns but feared missing the train's departure, and therefore decided against it. She even started dreading mealtimes because she didn't want to see the same people and menu each time.

Having nothing else to fill her idle time, she often spent most of it resting in her private room, daydreaming about what it would be like to live in Spruce Valley and be married to a sheriff. She imagined all the social gathering they'd attend together since he was such an important person in town. Emily smiled as she imagined herself dancing with the sheriff at charity balls or attending dinner with the Mayor at least once a week. She was excited about the idea of marrying someone so important. And when Josh needed to race from town to go after a criminal, she'd gush to all her friends over how proud she was of her husband. She'd no doubt make many jealous. The thought itself made her giggle with excitement.

Emily would also picture in her mind the type of house a sheriff must have. Since it was the West, she knew that Josh probably didn't own a home quite like the one she grew up in. She didn't think that manors were often seen in the West. But she'd be happy with a two-story home with plenty of spare bedrooms for guests who needed to sleep off a fun night over at their house. Emily would often smile with glee at the idea of throwing dinner parties for all the prestigious families in the area. She only hoped that the cook Josh employed would be skilled in the dishes she was used to. Emily knew that Southern food was very different from the rest of the country, but she'd be willing to help teach any cook about Georgia dishes if need be.

Emily had never really been excited about the idea of marriage. She simply knew that one day she wanted to be married and have a family of her own. The idea of childbirth terrified her because that is how her mother had died. And in Georgia, she'd been reassured by her family's physician that medicine had come a long way since then. But would this same type of medical treatment be available in Spruce Valley? She wasn't certain and would make sure to discuss this with Josh before they started trying for children.

And since Josh was such a famous sheriff, he would certainly aspire to one day become the Marshal of Montana. Then they could live closer to a large city and have all the creature comforts that she'd been used to. Emily reassured herself that she'd just have to deal with the minimum amenities in Spruce Valley while Josh continued rising up in law enforcement until he had the desired position that would allow them to relax for the rest of their lives. Emily was confident about her future with Josh, and now only hoped they'd one day grow to like each other.

JOSH SAT on the front porch of Frost's, his eyes focused on the road heading east out of town. He sat on a wooden bench, one that Mr. Frost had commissioned furniture maker Zachariah Welliver to make, so people could wait on the stagecoach. And as the sun slowly rose over the horizon, Josh sat in front of the mercantile waiting on the stagecoach to arrive for the day.

According to Emily's last telegram, she had already made her way to Wyoming. Josh knew that it wouldn't be much further for her to travel, after about two weeks, he could only imagine what kind of state she would arrive in. Being a Georgian socialite, Josh had a pretty good idea of what type of person Emily would be. She'd be surprised by Spruce Valley and probably compare it to Atlanta. And like the other mail-order-brides that had come before her, she'd either fall in love with the town and its people, or she'd hate it and perhaps come to resent Josh. But that was why she was only coming for a visit. There were no strings attached, and Josh felt quite comfortable with the current arrangement.

Even so, Josh sat on the bench anticipating the stagecoach with much nervousness. He was excited to finally get to meet Emily, even though they'd exchanged very few letters of communication. He had a gut feeling that Emily would be the type of person that he'd enjoy having as a wife. She'd shown him that she could be bold and therefore would at least be interesting to be with. He only hoped that she could deal with a simpler way of life that often required hard work to obtain what you truly wanted in life.

Though Josh had obtained his position in the community at a young age, he'd never turned down a challenge. He was excited to prove to everyone in town that he could be both a good and fair sheriff, but also someone they could rely on. He'd driven out criminals when they'd wandered into town and taken care of anyone else that would cause trouble. Sometimes disputes had to be settled between townsfolk, and he was okay with doing that type of humble work. Josh chuckled as he realized he was playing the middleman between the Slaters, and that was something he could be proud of too. He liked being the one people relied on when they needed help.

Josh hadn't written to his parents in southern Montana about Emily coming to meet him yet. He wanted to see how things went between them first before he wrote home. He'd grown up ranching with his father, but always dreamed of doing more. When a deputy's position had become available close to home, he'd taken it, even though he knew that his father needed the help at home. Josh had done his best to do the two jobs, but eventually ended up hiring someone to help out his father just so he wouldn't feel guilty when he took this sheriff job further away from home. As far as he knew, that ranch hand was still working for his father. It gave Josh some comfort to know that his parents were not on their own when it came to the ranch. He knew that they were getting on in years and one day would need to come stay with him in Spruce Valley.

Josh sighed, not liking the idea of seeing his parents away from the ranch. But he couldn't leave his job here in Spruce Valley and one day, he would have to convince them to sell the ranch and retire in Spruce Valley. And if he could marry and have a few children before then, he was certain the idea would appeal to his parents more, to be closer to their grandchildren.

All thoughts were pushed out of Josh's mind as dust began to stir on the road in the distance. The spring rains hadn't come, so it was still pretty dry on the roads, causing the dust cloud to rise up behind the stagecoach. The vehicle thundered down the road, the sound of hard-hitting hooves echoing as the stagecoach rumbled into town. It came to a sudden stop before the mercantile and Josh rose to his feet, bounding off the porch to open the carriage door for Emily so the driver could make his fast deliveries to Mr. Frost before continuing on.

"Welcome to Spruce Valley," Josh said as he stuck his head into the carriage. There on the velvet bench was a very road tired Emily. But she smiled happily at the news of finally arriving. She collected her purse and stepped down from the carriage with the help of the man that had opened the carriage door. She marveled at how handsome he was with his light brown hair and honey-colored eyes. The lopsided grin on his face did something to Emily; no man had ever been able to affect her in such a way.

"Thank you for your assistance. Are you valet?" Emily asked as she started to look in her purse for a few coins for the man. He laughed in response as he shook his head.

"No, Miss Emily Middleton. I am Sheriff Josh Ryder," he explained. Emily froze as Josh revealed his identity. She looked him up and down, from head to toe after realizing who he was. He wasn't dressed as finely as she would have assumed for a sheriff and for a moment, was puzzled by his simple Western shirt and jeans. A Stetson rested on his head, so she figured that at least he had good taste in hats.

"Forgive me, Sheriff. The long trip has left me less than presentable," Emily said as she put away her money. The driver dropped her trunk on the front porch of the store they'd come to a halt before, and her stomach tightened to see her own possessions treated so. Josh followed where she was looking and could only assume she was concerned about her things.

"Here, let me get that for you. I've arranged a room for you at the Honeywell Inn," Josh explained as he moved quickly to pick up her trunk. "Is this the only one?"

"Sure is, thank you," Emily replied. She was pleased to see that Josh was so thoughtful, and had planned ahead for her arrival. "I wanted to pack light and figured I'd only bring what I need and perhaps get what else I might need once I arrived."

"That's smart thinking," Josh said as he led her down the road. "The inn is right around the corner." Emily simply smiled and nodded. It felt good to walk after sitting and riding for so long. She took the time to really take in Josh's appearance, finding him very handsome and muscular. He lifted her trunk as though it weighed nothing.

As they walked together, Josh could hardly believe how beautiful Emily was. Though she looked tired from traveling, it didn't seem to take away from her natural beauty. She wore a gorgeous gown that Josh could only assume was made from the finest silks. He liked to think she'd dressed up for this occasion and appreciated that she took the time to do so. Her long, black hair hung around her shoulders in curls that Josh was curious would feel as silky as her gown. But he quickly pushed those thoughts out of his mind because he knew Emily was here to be his potential bride. She wasn't just another warm body to occupy his bed at night.

"Here's the inn," Josh said as he led her inside. "Bill Eckert is the owner and he'll be able to tend to your needs while you're visiting."

"I look forward to making his acquaintance," Emily replied. Mostly she was looking forward to a nice long bath and getting into a fresh gown. The inn appeared to be very minimal to Emily and she hoped that he had laundry services available.

"Hey there, Sheriff," said a man behind the counter that Emily could only assume was Bill.

"Hello, Mr. Eckert. I've brought Miss Middleton over from the depot to check in," Josh explained.

"Certainly, Sheriff," Bill replied as he turned and plucked a room key off the wall. Emily saw how there was only four and that the key Bill gave her was the only one being used. She figured that Spruce Valley didn't get many visitors. "I assume you'll take that up yourself?"

"Yes, Bill. I can show Miss Middleton the way and take the trunk upstairs," Josh replied, eager to spend as much time with Emily as possible.

"Oh, certainly you have an attendant who could carry the trunk for the good sheriff?" Emily spoke up, not wanting to cause her possible intended any more work.

"No, Miss Middleton. I manage the Honeywell Inn myself," Bill said, slightly embarrassed.

"That's quite okay. I don't mind," Josh said, understanding that Emily was more than likely used to a place where servants and attendants were at most places she visited. Emily thankfully only smiled kindly as she nodded.

"Welcome to the inn, Miss Middleton. I hope you enjoy your stay," Bill said before he left the counter and disappeared into a back room.

"I do hope I didn't offend him," Emily said as she followed Josh upstairs.

"Bill's always been a pretty private man, so don't worry," Josh replied, trying to reassure her. He figured that Emily would eventually learn that Spruce Valley wasn't like Atlanta at all. It might be a rude wake-up call for her, but he was confident that any independent woman with courage could adjust well to this small town.

"Here we are," Emily said as she found the room at the end of the hall and used the key Bill had given her to open it. She pushed open the door and stepped inside as Josh came through and set her trunk at the end of the bed. It was a small room with whitewashed walls that made the space feel bigger than what it was. It was nicely furnished, though not as nice as she was used to. But compared to the train and the stagecoach, it was a huge improvement.

"Thank you so much for bringing up my things," Emily said as she turned her attention to the sheriff. She flashed him her signature smile and saw the way he smiled at her in return.

"I'm always willing and able to help out when needed," Josh replied, mesmerized by her beautiful blue eyes and how they shined so brightly against her black hair. "How about a bite to eat once you get settled?" Emily's stomach rumbled and they both laughed at the sound.

"Food sounds like a lovely idea," Emily replied. "I just need to freshen up first. Where shall I meet you when I'm ready?"

"The Eatery is a small café at the back of Frost's mercantile. It was the place that the stagecoach stopped at," Josh explained.

"Easy enough," Emily said as Josh made his way towards the door.

"Alright then. I'll see you in a bit," Josh said absentmindedly as he pulled the door closed. He had a hard time not staring at Emily. She was certainly beautiful and would be turning a lot of heads in town. Josh couldn't help but whistle as he went down the hallway and then the stairs to reach the front of the inn.

"Got your hands full there, Sheriff," came Bill's voice. He'd returned from his small apartment at the back of the hotel and now stood once again at the counter. Josh stopped as he saw Bill at counter and slowly leaned over it, a dreamy look on his face.

"She sure is something, isn't she," Josh said, feeling pretty proud for having met Emily finally. He was certain that Bill would agree with him.

"Pardon me, Sheriff, but that woman only likes a certain type of man. And you're not it," Bill said straightforward. His words made Josh sober up right away.

"What are you talking about, Bill?" Josh asked, a bit annoyed by the innkeeper.

"Sheriff, I've seen it many times before," Bill said with a sigh. "A woman like that wants a man with loaded pockets so she doesn't have to lift a finger." Josh stared hard at Bill, trying to believe what he just heard.

"Look, I get she's from a big city, but that doesn't mean that Emily is the type of woman who would just be looking for a wealthy husband. She's very independent," Josh said, feeling like he needed to defend Emily's honor.

"Please, Sheriff, don't take me the wrong way," Bill said with his hands raised in front of him like he was a criminal surrendering to him. "I'm just looking out for the best person I know in town."

Josh chuckled then as he shook his head and straightened his posture. "Now you're just trying to sweet talk me," Josh said. "But I get what you're saying, Bill. I appreciate you looking out for me."

"Least I could do because you're always looking out for

the people of Spruce Valley," Bill said as Josh departed. Josh waved at Bill before leaving the inn. Something about Bill's words rubbed him the wrong way. He could understand that Bill was only watching out for him, but he didn't like the idea of anyone speaking disrespectfully of Emily. He only hoped that he didn't have any more trouble on Emily's first day in town.

CHAPTER 6

By the time Emily had taken a leisurely bath and dressed in a fresh gown, she was feeling like a completely new person. She'd finally made it to Spruce Valley, and all on her own without needing help from anyone. She felt a sense of accomplishment she'd never really felt before. Sure, she had taught many young ladies the proper way to act and talk during certain social settings, but nothing brought her as much satisfaction as she felt now for having taken care of herself. Now, as she made her way to the bottom level of the simple inn, she was looking forward to getting something to eat with the sheriff.

"All done with the tub, Miss Middleton?" Bill asked as she came down the stairs. Emily flashed him her signature smile and she could see the way his cheeks blushed. Emily was used to this type of reaction but didn't tease Bill any longer.

"I am, thank you," Emily said in parting. As she stepped out of the inn, she turned her eyes towards the mercantile the stagecoach had deposited her at. Emily took her time returning to the store. She took in the town around her, being able to see one end from the other from where she stood. She saw several men riding on horseback and so far hadn't seen a single carriage, or even a wagon. It made her wonder how folks got around without hired carriages. Just the idea of riding a horse didn't settle well with her, and she knew that she'd probably never leave Spruce Valley unless the sheriff had a small carriage for her.

Emily saw that there were a few important businesses in town. She noticed a clinic and felt relief that at least there was a local medical doctor. Emily wasn't surprised that there wasn't a hospital but thought that a clinic might do for child-birth. She also could see a furniture store and a women's seamstress shop at the far end of town. She looked forward to going into the store tomorrow. But for now, she needed a decent meal.

Stepping into Frost's mercantile, she took a moment to wander around the store. She was in need of a few things and was hoping she'd find them in stock. But the more she wandered around, the more she realized that most of the items for sale were food related, or some item needed to make some-thing else. Emily had never been in such a store and wondered if she'd ever need to purchase anything there.

Following her nose, Emily was able to locate The Eatery. Like the sheriff had explained, the café was rather small, but the smells coming from the place made Emily's mouth water. It all smelled like home-cooked food and that was something that Emily could use at that moment. Though there were a good number of patrons, she was able to skirt around the tables till she found Josh's table at the back. His Stetson was lowered over his face as though he'd been sleeping, and she wondered how long he'd been waiting on her.

Emily took a seat across from him, then leaned over the table and flicked back his hat with her fingers. She giggled when she realized he hadn't been sleeping at all.

"You surprised me," Emily confessed as she settled down into her chair.

"That is the whole point," Josh said with a wink. "Everyone always suspects that I'm sleeping and when the crook tries to sneak up on me, I surprise them in return."

"Seems like your sharing a trade secret with me," Emily said as she batted her eyelashes at Josh, trying to get his blood running hotter. His lopsided grin appeared once more, and she felt her own heart starting to beat faster as she took in his handsome looks.

"Why, are you interested in becoming my deputy?" Josh asked, enjoying the way Emily was trying to tease him.

"Certainly not, Sheriff. I can't imagine ever working a day in my life," Emily said with a laugh. But as Josh processed what she'd just said, he couldn't even force himself to laugh with her.

"Well, surely you thought of some employment to occupy yourself with once we are married?" Josh asked, trying to understand Emily's idea of marriage. Emily was surprised to hear this, trying to imagine why Josh would ever think she'd be able to work.

"Honestly, it's not something I've put much thought into," Emily said, trying to keep the peace. She didn't want to argue with the man she hoped to marry on their very first date. "In fact, I'd rather like to hear what your plans for the future are. Do you plan to ever run for State Marshal?" This time, Josh did laugh at the idea of him ever being a marshal.

"I plan to grow old and die in this town, Miss Middleton. Nothing on this earth could ever convince me to leave my position," Josh was able to explain once his mirth subsided. Emily stilled, not liking the idea that her future husband wasn't very ambitious. She was counting on him rising into a higher position that would ensure she'd never have to work a day in her life. But if Josh wasn't willing to be anything other than a sheriff, then perhaps she had to rethink her situation.

"Well, at least tell me what you'd recommend," Emily said as she turned her attention to the menu. "There are many dishes that I'm not familiar with."

"I see," Josh said, noticing the way Emily quickly changed the subject they were discussing. "I would suggest the meat-loaf if you've never had it before. Emmet makes an amazing meatloaf, and no one can beat Ella's mashed potatoes and gravy."

"Sounds delightful," Emily said with a smile, even though she didn't think having her food covered in gravy would be very appetizing. Perhaps she could imagine it was like grits and shrimp and still enjoy the dish.

When their waitress made her way to their table, Emily was surprised to see a female working in a café. She'd never dined in a place where a woman worked the front, always having waiters tend to her needs. She smiled at the woman as Josh introduced her to Nell. But the more the two women looked at each other, the more Emily thought she recognized Nell from somewhere long before.

"What can I get you two?" Nell asked in an uneasy voice. Josh quickly picked up on the waitress's tone of voice and started to look between the two of them. He could tell that they recognized each other.

"I'll have today's special, and Miss Middleton would like the meatloaf," Josh explained.

"And some tea, please," Emily added, her memory starting to come back to her.

"Right away, Miss," Nell said as she jotted down her notes and went immediately on her way.

"Do you know Nell or something?" Josh asked once the waitress was far away from the table that she wouldn't overhear their conversation.

"I have this feeling like I've seen her before, but not for a very long time," Emily explained as she watched Nell move across the room. "I almost want to say that she used to be a servant in my house and used to always pour the tea because she was so skilled at making the absolute perfect cup." Josh was surprised and looked at Nell, trying to imagine her working anywhere else but The Eatery. She'd come into town about the time Josh had taken up the position as sheriff.

"You remember why she left?" Josh asked. This was the first time he'd taken an interest in Nell and now he was dying to know her back story.

"I honestly have no idea," Emily admitted. "I simply remember her one day being gone and Father never mentioned where she'd gone."

Josh shook his head as he said, "Who would have thought that two ladies from the same place would have made their way to Spruce Valley?"

"I guess this world is really small after all," Emily said, remembering a literary quote she'd once read. As Nell came around and poured Emily a cup of tea, she remembered the woman more clearly. She didn't mention this to Nell, thinking that now wasn't the time or place to speak about such things, but as she took a sip of the tea, she couldn't help but sigh deeply.

"As delicious as I remember," Emily said as she smiled kindly up at the woman. Nell simply nodded before walking off again.

"Doesn't look like Nell enjoys remembering," Josh observed.

"Yes, I would have to agree with you on that," Emily said.

"Are you saying you're a good observer?" Josh asked, his interest in Emily piquing.

"I wasn't lying when I said I won that poker game," Emily said as she smiled at Josh over the rim of her teacup. "It's easy to play when you're watching the players more than the cards."

"Seems like we should plan a time to play a game or two sometime," Josh suggested, feeling like it was so easy to flirt with her. He could easily tell that she was the type of young lady that was often flirted with and that she could handle her own in a crowd of gentlemen.

"Just tell me when and where and I'll be there," Emily agreed. "I never back down from a good challenge."

"And nor do I," Josh said, feeling like Emily would be the type of woman that would give him a run for his money.

When their food arrived, they settled into mutual silence as they ate. Emily found the meatloaf to be a hardy meal, but one that she could easily enjoy. The flavors were bold and she couldn't deny how hungry she was after eating mostly stale bread and salted meat for almost two weeks. By the time they were done, she had completely cleaned her plate.

"I would have never thought a woman such as yourself could eat me under the table," Josh said with a chuckle. Emily blushed, knowing how much she'd eaten was very unladylike. She was just so hungry that she couldn't help herself.

"I have to admit that I did surprise myself," Emily replied softly.

Josh quickly realized his error and said, "I like a woman who can hold her own and isn't afraid to show her true feelings." Emily chuckled at that response, glad to find Josh so humorous.

"Well, at this time I think I could use a long rest. After being without a proper bed for two weeks, I'm eager to finally get to use one," Emily said as she patted her lips with a napkin and rose from the table. "I'll be sure to come pay you a visit tomorrow at the Sheriff's Office."

"I'd be delighted to see you tomorrow then," Josh replied as he dipped his hat towards her. She winked at him, causing his blood to run warm. As he watched her walk out of The Eatery, turning several heads, Josh thought he was the luckiest man alive to have been given the opportunity to court such a lovely woman. Josh was always more attractive to women with dark hair, and Emily seemed to be the full package, with a tall, slim frame and elegant manners.

But as Josh fished out some money out of his pocket to pay for their meal, Bill's words came back to haunt him. He wondered if there could be any truth to them, especially as he thought about what Emily had said about work. Josh wanted a wife that could be his equal, not some woman he'd have to take care of. He expected his wife to work just as much as he did, and he knew he couldn't support the type of lifestyle that Emily might have been used to back in Atlanta. As Josh waited for the bill, and thought more about his interaction with Emily today, he could tell that there was a chemistry between them but couldn't say if Emily would one day become his wife.

EMILY WAS STARTING to fret as she returned to the inn. She wasn't completely pleased with everything she'd learned about Josh. She didn't know how much he currently made a year as the small town's sheriff but was certain that it was nowhere near what she'd been expecting. Emily hadn't felt that it was the right time to talk about his current financial situation but felt pressed to do so soon after everything she'd been through with her father. She also knew that at some point she'd have to come clean to the sheriff, if their relationship did start to progress.

As Emily entered the inn, she approached the counter and asked Bill for a few sheets of writing paper. She wanted to write Cynthia right away to at least let her know that she'd arrived in Spruce Valley safely and to share her current insight on the sheriff.

"That will be five cents," Bill said with an uneasy smile. He felt intimidated by Miss Middleton and didn't know how she would react to being asked to purchase the paper.

56

"Of course," Emily said as she took out a few coins from her purse and gave them to Bill as he handed her the writing paper. "Thank you." With the paper in hand, she turned from the counter and made her way up the stairs to her room. She didn't want Bill to think that she was ungrateful, so she had willingly paid for the paper because she was certain the Sheriff was paying for her room. And since Emily could tell that the inn didn't receive many patrons, she would have to expect Bill to charge her for almost everything.

Emily sighed heavily as she made it back to her room, making sure to lock the door securely behind her. Alone, she felt like she could let her guard down as she let down her hair and allowed it to hang around her shoulders. She took to the writing desk in the room and began to pen her long letter to Cynthia. She figured she'd have to return to Frost's to mail the letter since she hadn't spotted a post office. But Emily didn't worry too much about what she was going to do next. For now, she simply wrote all she'd learned and discovered about Spruce Valley and Josh Ryder to her dearest friend.

Not wanting to worry Cynthia, Emily did her best to write about everything in a positive light. After all, the small town was a cute little place, and everyone had seemed to be friendly thus far. And, Josh was a very handsome man who was easy to tease. She certainly looked forward to having the opportunity to play cards with him and wondered how daring the Sheriff was when he was supposed to be the main role model for all the town's people. The very thought made her smile as she penned her letter.

Emily even wrote about how surprised she was to see Nell working at the café. Emily described first her shock over seeing a female waiter, and then coming to discover the woman used to work for her father as a servant. Emily wondered if Cynthia would remember her for the woman who made the best cup of tea either one of them ever had. A part of Emily wanted to know why Nell had left her father's staff and came all the way out to Spruce Valley. She always enjoyed a good story and felt like Nell would have a juicy one to tell her, even though the woman didn't look too pleased to see her.

After Emily had finished her letter, she changed into a simple day gown and out of the pale-yellow silk gown she'd worn to simply show-off for Josh. In something a little more comfortable, Emily crawled underneath the covers of the bed and let out a sigh of relief. The bed was small, yet comfortable. It had been so long since Emily had the pleasure of sleeping in a real bed that she felt her body relax immediately. She reasoned that she could possibly sleep till tomorrow, the sun already passing noon.

As Emily closed her eyes and held the pillow close to her body, she wondered what she was going to do about her present situation. If she and Josh did marry, would he really expect her to work? She didn't have any skills that she could turn into some sort of employment, and the very idea didn't settle well with her. After all, she was a Middleton and none of the women in her family had ever worked. But as Emily drifted off to sleep, she couldn't help but wonder what sort of life she could possibly have with the Sheriff, and what she'd be willing to do to obtain stability in her life once more.

CHAPTER 7

When the morning came, Emily did her best to stay positive. She had plans to visit the women's seamstress shop that morning to have proper gowns made for her, since she had brought so little with her. Shopping for new gowns always cheered her up and Emily was determined to have a good day.

After she rose from bed, Emily did her best to wash up and dress herself. After having to do it for over a month now, Emily was starting to get used to the task. She even had practiced doing her own hair and now wore her long black hair pinned up to the top of her head. With it being spring, she wore light fabrics so she wouldn't get too hot as the day progressed. Viewing her reflection in the small looking glass in the room, Emily felt pleased with her ability to not only dress properly, but also do her hair.

Once Emily felt ready enough for the day, she collected her purse and her letter to Cynthia, then made her way out of her room, locking the door behind her. Emily thought she could get a bite to eat at The Eatery since it was the only restaurant in town. Perhaps she could even meet some of the local townsfolk and maybe even get a chance to talk to Nell about why she left her previous position back in Georgia. She also liked the idea of talking with someone from home.

Emily waved at Bill as he stood at the counter. He seemed to be reading a novel and she didn't want to disturb him. Once outside, she was greeted with the morning sun. Emily had to admit that Spruce Valley was a quaint town. It might not be as flashy as Atlanta, a whole lot more convenient, but there was a small town charm that had settled over the place. In the distance, Emily could hear the sound of a church bell, and she was able to see all the children racing towards it. Emily figured that the church must also act as a school building. Emily had always been privately tutored so the idea of attending school with others intrigued her.

Having nothing better to do, Emily walked through town and approached the church, curious to see the children attending their lessons from the day. As she approached the church, she could hear all sorts of happy chatter as the children assembled and got ready for their day. As Emily walked up the stairs of the church and peered in, the pews were filled with local children of all ages. And at the front stood a woman.

Emily was surprised as she looked all around the church. There wasn't a man present, and Emily had never heard of a female schoolteacher. Spruce Valley seemed to be full of many surprises where women obviously held different positions.

Perhaps there were no educated men in Spruce Valley and that is why a woman had been selected for the position.

Seeming to be noticed, the woman at the front of the church shushed the children and gave them their morning math problems for them to figure out on their clay tablets before approaching Emily. She smiled kindly at the woman approaching her, hoping she wasn't interrupting the day's lesson.

"Good morning, Miss. Is there something I can help you with?" the teacher asked kindly.

"Forgive me if I'm interrupting. I've never seen a school like this and was simply interested," Emily explained. "My name is Emily Middleton. I just arrived yesterday."

"Ah, I see. Well, my name is Mrs. Jenny Crawford. I'm the schoolteacher," Jenny explained.

Emily could see that Jenny was far along in her pregnancy and asked, "When are you expecting your baby?"

Jenny chuckled as she ran her hands over her midsection. "It seems like any day now," Jenny explained as she looked down at herself. "I was hoping this little girl or guy would wait till this summer when school is out, but it doesn't seem that way."

"Do you have a teacher to replace you for when you'll be recovering with your baby?" Emily asked, curious to know how the school system worked in Spruce Valley.

Jenny shook her head with a sorrowful expression on it. "I'm guessing you're not from around here because you'd already know that I'm the only schoolteacher," Jenny explained.

"I'm from Atlanta, Georgia," Emily explained. "I was

privately tutored so I never had the opportunity to attend lessons with others." Emily looked around the church and smiled to see all the eager students looking her way instead of on their mathematics.

"I see why this would interest you so," Jenny said. "Would you care to join us for the morning lesson?"

"Oh, I wouldn't want to impose," Emily said quickly, surprised by the woman's offer.

"You wouldn't be at all," Jenny reassured her. "It would be good to have another adult in the room to help me keep an eye on the more rebellious ones." Jenny then looked behind her, the students turning around quickly and focusing on their work once more as giggles swarmed across the room. Emily couldn't help but giggle with them.

"I need to mail a letter and grab something to eat first, but then I'll come back to observe for a bit," Emily agreed, thinking it might be fun to help out in a classroom setting.

"Sounds like a plan. I look forward to seeing you again after a bit, Miss Middleton," Jenny said before she turned and began to address the students. Emily stood for a moment and watched as Jenny flawlessly started to review the many math problems she'd distributed for the different ages. Emily was certainly impressed by her ability to teach so many ages at once and looked forward to seeing the students later. But first, she needed food in her stomach.

Emily descended the stairs of the church and made her way back over to the mercantile. There, she visited with Mr. Frost for a few minutes as she asked him to mail her letter. He seemed like he was a very sweet older man who enjoyed talking. Since Emily enjoyed a good bit of gossip, she imagined talking Mr. Frost's ear off when there weren't so many people in the shop. After being introduced to Mrs. Frost, she made her way around to The Eatery to order some sort of breakfast.

Emily waved at Nell as she sat down at a table. It didn't seem to be all that busy that morning, and Emily wondered if that was because not everyone was awake yet, or if she was simply the one seeming to be running behind. Either way, she was looking forward to getting something to eat and perhaps speaking with Nell privately.

"Good morning, Miss Middleton. How can I help you?" Nell asked as she came over to her table.

"What would you suggest, Nell? I'm not very familiar with the cuisine out here," Emily admitted. Nell smirked as she nodded, thinking the daughter of Mr. Middleton was far from home. She didn't understand why Emily was here, and she only hoped it wasn't to see her, in particular. After seeing Emily with the Sheriff, she suspected that Emily had come as a mail-order-bride. But since Nell knew how wealthy the Middleton's were, she couldn't ever see Emily in that position either.

"Scrambled eggs, bacon, and toast are what's most popular. Nothing like the poached eggs and fresh fruit of Georgia," Nell said with her hands on her hips. Emily knew without a shadow of a doubt now that Nell was the servant who used to work for her father. And as Emily looked around the café and saw only one other customer, she dared to ask the question that had been on her mind since last night.

"Nell, what on earth are you doing in Spruce Valley? Why did you ever leave?" Emily asked as she straightened her posture. She wasn't ashamed of her question at all and was dreadfully curious. Nell sighed as she settled into the chair across from Emily, folding her arms over her.

"Miss Middleton, do you really want to hear the truth?" Nell asked. "You won't like it."

"Nell, I don't ever plan to go back to Atlanta so it can't hurt anything now," Emily explained. She wasn't ready to tell Nell the real reason why she had left Atlanta and what had happened to her father's business. But it was easy to say that she never wanted to go back to Georgia. As she watched Nell closely, observing her every moment, she could tell that the woman was surprised.

"Is your father with you? Does he plan to come to Spruce Valley any time soon?" Nell asked as she narrowed her eyes at the young lady. The last thing she wanted was another confrontation with Mr. Middleton.

"No," Emily said as she turned her eyes away from Nell for a moment. She let out a heavy sigh, wondering whatever would become of her father. He'd never been very affectionate, but she still wondered about him from time to time. Her response only made Nell more curious, but she decided not to press the issue until Emily felt comfortable enough to talk to her about it.

"In that case, I can tell you that the reason I left employment at your household was because your father was attracted to me," Nell explained slowly. "I didn't return his feelings in any way, so when I refused to be with him intimately, he fired me immediately without giving me any references." Emily looked up at Nell then, clearly shocked to hear this. "I couldn't stay in Atlanta after that, in fear of what type of reputation I then had. So I hopped on the train heading West and never looked back."

Emily was stunned by the explanation. She'd never heard from any of the other staff being pressured by her father, and though she could admit that Nell was a beautiful woman, she couldn't imagine her father sinking that low. But after all the shady business deals that her father had made, she shouldn't be overly surprised by his past behaviors.

"I'm so sorry to hear that, Nell," Emily eventually said. "You are the best tea maker I've ever known, and though I'm new to Spruce Valley, I can honestly say I'm pleased to see you again." Nell smiled slightly as she nodded. She was often complimented by her skills at making a good cup of tea.

"But why are *you* in Spruce Valley?" Nell then asked, leaning forward over the table so that Emily could feel comfortable speaking to her. Emily bit her lower lip, wondering how much she should tell Nell. After all, her former servant and come clean to her.

"I'm here as a mail-order-bride for the Sheriff. Let's just say that my father ruined my reputation, too," Emily explained. Nell raised her eyebrows at hearing this, even more curious than before.

"Well, it's none of my business, but I hope you'll make Josh happy. He's the best of the best, and deserves as much," Nell said as she got up from the table. "I'll go make you a cup of tea and fix you a decent breakfast."

"Thank you," was all Emily said in parting, hopeful that Nell would order her something she'd like. She was eager to eat something so she could return to the church to observe the students. And the idea of being of some sort of use to Mrs. Crawford intrigued her.

Emily couldn't help but think of her father as she enjoyed her breakfast. Egg whites had been separated from the yoke to create a light and fluffy scrambled egg, paired with a few sausage rolls. It was a light breakfast that Emily was used to and appreciated Nell's consideration. After all, she knew so few people in town thus far and could always use a friend. Emily thought how strange her life had turned after learning that her father was now penniless and that she would soon have a tarnished reputation. Even though she'd just arrived in Spruce Valley, she thought of traveling all the way here as something unimaginable. Yet, she'd done it, and survived the aftermath of her father's failing business.

After breakfast, Emily made sure to give Nell a decent sized tip. The tea had been as excellent as ever, and though Emily did not have a large fortune, she felt that Nell deserved to be recognized for her continuous service to her. As they said parting words, Emily left The Eatery and made her way through town and back to the church.

By the time she arrived, the children had been released for a short break from their morning studies. Emily came to stand next to Jenny in the school yard as children raced around, playing tag or hopscotch. It filled Emily with joy to see so many little ones happy. Emily hadn't had much time for playing growing up since her father had made her education a vital part of her upbringing. She'd been groomed since birth to be married off to a wealthy man to continue the Middleton traditions. Now, she felt at a loss of what her fate would actually be.

"So, what brings you to Spruce Valley, Miss Middleton?" Jenny asked after a bit. They'd watched the children play together, but Jenny was very curious about this newcomer.

"I answered Sheriff Ryder's mail-order-bride ad," Emily explained with a kind smile. "I've come to see if we'll make a good match." Jenny looked at her then, surprised by the news.

"I didn't know that the good Sheriff had placed an ad," Jenny remarked. "Well, I'm certainly glad you are here. I always thought that Josh deserved to meet a nice young lady and settle down." Emily chuckled, feeling like that was everyone's opinion of Josh. She was at least glad to hear that he was so well liked.

"Well, we shall see how things go," Emily said.

"And what type of employment are you looking for now that you are here?" Jenny asked. Emily was as surprised by her words as she had been when Josh had asked her the same thing last night. Emily refrained from replying right away, realizing that women worked all sorts of different positions in Spruce Valley. Were all the women expected to work?

"I haven't given it much consideration to be honest. It's a new idea for me," Emily explained, feeling a bit embarrassed.

"That is understandable. After all, you only arrived yesterday," Jenny said, sensing Emily's unease. By the fine fabrics that Emily's light green gown was made from, Jenny assumed that Emily was from a very wealthy family. The idea of working must be foreign to her.

"I am surprised to see so many women in important positions. I was surprised to see Nell as a waiter when I've only seen men in that position, and all my tutors were also men,"

Emily explained. Jenny chuckled as she rubbed her pregnant belly.

"Then you'll be further surprised to hear that Spruce Valley's mayor is also a woman," Jenny said. She was correct, because Emily was instantly shocked upon hearing this.

"How on earth was a woman elected to such an important position?" Emily asked, very curious to learn this. If a woman could be mayor, then perhaps she could one day also hold a very important position in town.

"Well, her late husband was the last mayor, and when he passed away, Delphina Stavros simply took up his spot," Jenny explained. "She does a fine job and even convinced the telegram company to run lines all the way out here to Spruce Valley. She has a daughter she looks after as well as a few grandchildren, but she does her best to honor her husband's memory." Emily took a few moments to think about Jenny's words, thinking how honorable that was of Mrs. Stavros.

"And none of the men have said anything about the woman mayor?" Emily asked, curious to learn how long Mrs. Stavros had been in the position.

"I'm sure a few have tried, but Mrs. Stavros is a force to be reckoned with. Here I am, a married woman and pregnant, but yet I'm still teaching. She's been mayor for almost a decade now and I don't think any man would dare try to get in her way, and she makes sure that us women aren't bothered by men and their sore opinions," Jenny said with a chuckle. Emily was very curious about the woman and looked forward to meeting her.

Soon after, Jenny called all the children back into the church. Emily joined them and assisted Jenny in instructing the students on their words for the day. Emily particularly liked helping the younger children write their letters and words, encouraging them to sound out each letter in order to read. She enjoyed seeing their smiling faces. Jenny was impressed by the way Emily was interacting with the children and how easily she taught them. An idea came into her mind then and she wondered when she could speak to Emily about it in the near future.

After a while, Emily said goodbye to Jenny and the students. She wanted to visit the women's seamstress shop, and since it might take a while to be properly fitted and for the gowns to be designed, Emily knew that it was better to head over now before the day got away from her. After all, she told Josh that she'd come to visit him as well and wanted to leave room in her day for that. The children said happy goodbyes. Emily promised to come visit again soon as she left the church and walked down the road to the other side of town, till she reached the women's seamstress shop.

As Emily entered, she was pleasantly surprised by the elegant design of the shop. It was clearly decorated for women and reminded her of several other shops back in Atlanta. It was nice to see something familiar, and as she approached a short rack of pre-made gowns, she realized that not only had they been designed smartly, but they were much like the gowns she'd worn back in Georgia.

"Hello," came a woman's voice, drawing Emily's attention to the front counter. "Can I help you with something?" Emily smiled as she approached the woman with auburn hair.

"I've come in to have some gowns designed. I was hoping for a fitting, then a consultation," Emily explained. The woman smiled kindly at her as she began to observe Emily closely, no doubt sizing her up in her mind already.

"I'd be happy to assist you. My name is Fiona Murtaugh, and I fix and repair garments," the woman explained. "But Mrs. Slater, the owner and seamstress, has taught me how to take measurements. I can do that for you and send them to her since she's on bed rest."

"My name is Emily Middleton. Since the seamstress isn't well, is she currently not taking any orders?" Emily asked, feeling a little deflated at the thought.

Fiona smiled at her as she said, "Well, Lucy is supposed to be resting but that woman can't sit still to save her life. Though she's agreed to stay in bed, she's still making gowns at home with her business partner, Martha Jenkins."

"How nice that all three of you are working together to manage this shop," Emily admitted. "Coming all the way from Georgia, it's nice to see something a little familiar."

Fiona nodded, knowing just how Emily felt. "I'm originally from Boston myself," Fiona said. "I came out here last year as a mail-order-bride and was so impressed by everything that Lucy and Martha have been able to accomplish on their own." Hearing Fiona's words, she was instantly curious about the woman. She remembered how Josh had explained there were other mail-order-brides, but as she observed Fiona closely, she could tell that this young lady was also a socialite.

"The one thing that Spruce Valley has shown me is that women really can do anything. Just now I learned that the mayor is a woman," Emily said. Fiona giggled, covering her mouth with the back of her hand. It was a clear sign that Fiona was from a wealthy family and she was dying to know why she'd come out to the West. Had her family also become penniless? But by the fine fabrics of her dress, Emily would have guessed that Fiona was still wealthy. Perhaps she'd married a wealthy gentleman as well…?

"Yes, Spruce Valley has lots of surprises," Fiona admitted. "I think that's because the people here are so interesting and hardworking. This might sound funny, but I didn't feel alive until I started working for Lucy and Martha. I might have been raised with every luxury, but my true purpose wasn't discovered until I came here." Emily was startled by her words, trying to imagine ever finding pleasure from working. She dreaded the idea of hard labor and tried to see Fiona's perspective on life. She could only guess that her previous life had been so dreadful that she enjoyed working now that she was in Spruce Valley.

"I'll have to take your word on that, Fiona," Emily said, wanting to turn her attention over to the gowns she wanted to have ordered. She wanted something nice for her day gown, and a few evening gowns for when she would go on dates with Josh or attending other important social gatherings.

"Well, that's enough about me. How about we get you measured, and you can tell me about the gown you'd like to have designed," Fiona said, sensing Emily's restlessness. Emily smiled kindly and nodded as she followed Fiona back to the fitting room.

"I was hoping to have a few gowns made," Emily explained. "I want something nicer for the day and evening."

"Well, there are all types of different fabrics to choose from," Fiona explained as she went about measuring Emily's body with a tape measure. She wrote clearly on a piece of paper, planning to bring it to Lucy that evening on her way home from town. "You'll no doubt want something breathable for everyday wear since the weather is warming up."

"That would be ideal. I just want to make sure it's good quality as well," Emily explained.

"Are these gowns more for show or work?" Fiona asked as she moved around Emily, moving her arms out to the side so she could measure her waist and bust.

"I would say show. I don't work," Emily said pointedly. Fiona suspected that Emily must be new in town. Though she had met most of the townspeople after having moved to Spruce Valley to marry her husband, Eddie, and started working in town, she figured that perhaps Emily had come to visit with some of her family that Fiona had simply not met yet.

"Will you be staying in Spruce Valley for long? I want to let Lucy know how soon she needs to have the gowns made," Fiona said.

"Spruce Valley is my new home," Emily explained. "I've come to be a mail-order-bride for Sheriff Ryder." Fiona almost dropped the measuring tape after hearing this.

"My goodness, how fascinating! I had no idea that the Sheriff had placed an ad," Fiona admitted. "He's one of the kindness men I know. If it wasn't for the Sheriff, I wouldn't be here right now." Fiona then took the time to explain her story and how she'd come to live in Spruce Valley after being kidnapped by train robbers and then rescued by the Sheriff, Eddie, and their close friends.

"Oh, Fiona, I'm so sorry to hear that. It must have been absolutely terrifying," Emily said as she looked Fiona directly in the eyes. She wanted the woman to know she was speaking very genuinely. Emily could also admit that her travels to Spruce Valley were mild compared to what Fiona had to go through to get here.

"Well, that's all behind us now. I don't often think of it because I'm so happy with Eddie," Fiona said with a grand smile. Emily could tell she was speaking the truth and hoped that one day she could also feel that type of happiness.

Emily and Fiona spent almost two hours together as they went over gown designs and fabric. Emily was enjoying her time with the other mail-order-bride, learning more about her time here in Spruce Valley, but also realizing that the woman had good taste. Emily could easily see herself becoming good friends with Fiona, the woman often reminding her of her own dearest friend, Cynthia.

After their business had come to an end, Fiona took the time to write up the final bill. It was the most expensive bill Fiona had ever written up and figured that Emily also came from a wealthy family. Though she didn't think the gowns would be fitting for life in Spruce Valley, she wasn't going to argue with the woman who was going to pay for the gowns.

"Here you are," Fiona said as she handed the bill to Emily. Emily nodded as she reviewed it.

"Everything looks in order. Have the bill sent over to the Sheriff for processing," Emily said as she handed it back to Fiona. Fiona was startled to hear this, thinking this large bill wouldn't be something Josh could handle. Only a very successful businessman would be able to take care of this. But not wanting to cause trouble, Fiona only nodded. But after Emily left the shop, Fiona couldn't help but have a bad feeling about this situation. Fiona could tell that Emily was a very nice girl, but she didn't want the Sheriff to be taken advantage of.

Fiona gathered her things and left the shop, locking the door behind her. She then quickly made her way to the Sheriff's Office, needing to explain to Josh what had just happened before she would be willing to take the designs to Lucy.

CHAPTER 8

*J*osh was seething with anger after speaking with Fiona. He'd done his best not to show his emotions as Fiona came to him and explained how Emily had ordered an expensive bill of gowns and had told Fiona to bring him the bill. He'd taken the bill from Fiona, saying that he'd have to discuss things with Emily before approving the order. Fiona had smiled uneasily at him after agreeing and quickly left him alone since she needed to get back to the shop. And the moment Fiona had left, Josh had tightened his fists so tightly that he tore the piece of paper that detailed everything Emily had tried to order and then leave him with the cost.

Josh did his best to get his anger under control as he thought about how to best handle this situation. He wasn't sure if Emily was trying to test him, but he certainly wasn't going to give in and just waste his savings so that Emily could have some new clothes. He'd need to talk to Emily about this matter right away and hopefully do it in a way that she'd understand that he was never going to tolerate this type of behavior.

As Josh left the Sheriff's Office, he went to look for Emily. He went straightaway to the inn, thinking she'd be there and perhaps resting. But as he started walking in that direction, he saw her in the distance, standing on the edge of town and looking out into the large expanse of land that stretched on for as long as the eye could see. He quickly walked over to her but didn't say anything right away as she leaned against a tree and simply stared off into the distance.

Even though Josh was angry at her, he couldn't deny how beautiful she was. She was wearing a fitting gown that showed off the best parts of her curvy figure. It was her beauty that had instantly intrigued Josh, but he hoped that he hadn't been wrong about her good character.

"Emily," Josh said, pulling the woman out of her daydream. She turned to him quickly, surprised to see him when she'd just been thinking about him. She had been curious about what Spruce Valley looked like outside of town and she'd become preoccupied by taking it all in. She couldn't believe how far and wide the land stretched with not a single building or home dotting the landscape. She was thinking how glad she was to be in town and not stuck in the middle of nowhere.

"Josh, it's so good to see you," Emily said as she settled her nerves and smiled at the Sheriff. "I was so captivated by the beautiful scenery that I lost myself in thought." Josh nodded, understanding because he often enjoyed taking long rides out of town on his mare to simply take in the beauty of Spruce Valley this time of year.

"It sure is lovely out here," Josh agreed. Then taking a deep breath, he withdrew the crumbled-up piece of paper in his pocket and handed it to Emily. "Fiona brought this over to me. To say I was surprised is an understatement."

Emily took the piece of paper and looked down at it to see that it was the bill from the women's seamstress shop. Her brows furrowed as she looked back up at Josh, trying to understand his surprise and why he'd crumbled up the paper.

"Is there some sort of problem?" Emily asked. Josh was very concerned by her words as he tried to think of the best way to explain things to her. He figured that being blunt would be the best thing in this situation.

"Emily, I can't afford to purchase all of these gowns for you. Perhaps one, when it comes time to marry," Josh explained. "If you want new gowns, you'll have to pay for them yourself or have your father send you some money." He didn't like talking to Emily like this, but she needed to have a solid idea of his character. Emily was even more perplexed by his words as she fought to keep her temper at bay.

"Josh, I can't just ask my father for money..." Emily said, knowing that the time had come to tell Josh the whole truth. "The reason I replied to your ad is because my father lost everything in bad business deals. The day I left Atlanta for here, I ran away from an empty home that had been torn down to just a shell. My father was nowhere to be seen."

Josh certainly wasn't expecting this from Emily. He had his suspicions about why she wanted to marry him, or why she had been so eager to come straight away to Spruce Valley, and now the big picture was becoming clear to him. He ran his fingers through his hair, realizing just how much trouble Emily was going to be for him.

"I'm sorry to hear about your father, Emily," Josh said, trying to be sympathetic. "It must have been hard on you, and it explains why you were so eager to come here." Emily nodded, doing her best to keep her tears at bay.

"I didn't mean to be so deceiving, Josh, but I didn't want to tell you some sob story just to convince you to marry me. I honestly want to see if we'll do well together first," Emily said.

"And if we don't? What will you do then?" Josh asked, his temper starting to rise again. He wasn't keen on the idea that Emily hadn't told him the entire truth.

"I have a small fortune that I brought with me. I don't have a solid plan, but I really am hoping that things will work out between us," Emily said, straightening her posture. "I figured your salary as a sheriff will be suitable for the both of us." Josh shouldn't have, but he couldn't help but laugh at her idea of their married life. He shook his head, trying to figure out what Emily's end goal was with marrying him.

"Emily, I hate to break this to you, but if you want things like new gowns, you'll have to find employment and pay for them yourself," Josh said point blank. "As I'm sure you can tell, women need to make their own way here in Spruce Valley. I'm not some rich man who can sustain your previous way of life."

Emily was trying to keep her composure as she listened to everything Josh was telling her. She couldn't believe what she was hearing. She'd placed so much of her future on marrying the Sheriff and not having to worry about working. But if he couldn't take care of a simple gown order, something her father had no issue paying in the past, then perhaps the Sheriff was as poor as her father was now.

"I've never considered working before, ever in my life," Emily said, tears coming to her eyes. "I honestly dread the idea."

"Well, I understand how this may all seem different to you, Emily. But if things are going to work out between us, then I need to be able to respect my wife. And I can't do that if you're not willing to find some sort of employment to help support our family," Josh said. A part of him felt terrible for being so straightforward with Emily, but the other side of him thought that this type of explanation was exactly what Emily needed if she was going to survive on her own. In her current condition, Josh wasn't sure if they had a future together if she was going to rely on him for everything.

Crumbling the gown order into her hands, she threw it at Josh's feet and quickly walked around him. She hurried back to the inn, tears streaming down her cheeks. She felt embarrassed for having come all this way to be his wife and even more livid at Josh for the way he'd spoken to her. She wasn't some child that needed scolding. How dare he speak to her as such?

Emily was thankful that no one saw her as she entered the inn. And even more grateful that Bill wasn't at the counter. She took the stairs two at a time till she reached the second floor and could disappear into her room. She was breathing heavily from all the fast movement that her chest heaved up and down as she tried to catch her breath. She flopped down upon the bed as she pulled a pillow close to her and buried her face in it, letting out all of her frustration.

Emily cried for what seemed like hours. She was alone, afraid, and completely helpless. She'd placed so much hope and trust in Josh that she couldn't imagine what she was going to do now. She certainly couldn't ever work, even though she saw how many women in the community held important jobs. She'd never been raised to work, only to marry a wealthy man so she'd never have to worry about money. But as she thought about the small fortune she had with her, she knew that it wouldn't be able to sustain her for the rest of her life.

Eventually, Emily was able to calm down. She thought of Josh, thinking how handsome and kind he'd been to her thus far. Though he wasn't willing to sustain her in their marriage, he still had a lot of good qualities. Though she was still furious with him, she couldn't deny her attraction to him. As she drifted off to sleep, she was at battle with her emotions as she thought about how ridiculous the idea of working was.

JOSH CERTAINLY FELT terrible as he watched Emily storm off. He wanted to go after her but didn't know what he could say to her at this moment. She needed to understand how important it was that she worked, but it was clear to him that she didn't like the idea at all. Josh picked up the crumpled piece of paper she'd thrown at his feet and put it in his pocket. He hated the idea of breaking her heart or making her feel more miserable than she must already be. Now that he understood why Emily had agreed to come to Spruce Valley and why she was so eager to do so, he tried to think just how upset she had to have been to leave behind everything that was familiar to her to go somewhere completely new with the knowledge she could never return to her home.

Josh sighed heavily as he turned and made his way to the livery stables. He wanted to have a long talk with his best friend but knew that the doctor had already left the clinic for the day. Not wanting to try to talk to Emily right now, Josh collected his mare from the stables before heading out of town and to the Slater Ranch.

Josh always enjoyed the long ride out to the ranch. The road cut through the landscape, skirting around a dense forest before opening up to the never-ending expansion of land. Needing to release his own frustrations over Emily's unrealistic views of their marriage together, he set his mare off at a fast gallop, feeling the wind whipping by his face as the roar of it sounded in his ears. He loved the thrill of riding at such high speeds, sometimes reminding him of previous chases he gave when catching criminals that were trying to get away.

As he approached the ranch, Josh pulled on the reins to slow down his mare. She trotted down the lane to the ranch house, happy to have been able to get a good exercise for the day. Normally Josh took his mare out to do some patrolling around town, but it had been a while since they'd last moved at those speeds. It was exactly what they both needed as Josh pulled the mare to a stop before the house and dismounted, tying the reins to the front hitching post before heading inside.

The Slater household was in complete uproar, as normal. Everyone was sitting down at the dining table, or at least trying to as fathers chased their little ones around in order to get them settled at the table. Josh just shook his head as he took off his Stetson and hung it by the door. Ever since Lucy had arrived at the ranch, she'd insisted on cooking every meal for the ranch hands. And now that two of the ranch hands had married, their numbers had increased, making every meal almost a comical act.

"Good to see ye, Sheriff," came Lucy's voice at the head of the table. Since she'd been on bed rest, she'd been taking it easy. Though she enjoyed cooking, she turned that task over to Gray and his wife Martha. Gray had experience cooking for the ranch hands and often filled in for Lucy, even though he was the foreman and put in long hours at the ranch. But as Josh heard him whistling in the kitchen, Josh knew that the man didn't mind one bit.

"Hello there, Lucy. Care for one more?" Josh said with a chuckle.

"Ah, ye always know yer welcome here anytime," Lucy said with a smile. "And ye can tell me what's been happening in town." Josh stilled then as he thought about Emily. Lucy could see that something was bothering the Sheriff. And even in all the commotion of the evening meal, Lucy put her focus on her friend.

"Well, me and Emily have come to a crossroads. She gave me some insight today on what she had been expecting by coming out here and getting married to me," Josh said. As everyone came around the table to get ready for dinner, they listened to Josh's story with much concern.

"I can see her point of view, Josh. Remember, I was a debutante meself," Lucy said as she looked towards her husband. He sat beside her on the bench with their daughter on his lap. She'd recently turned two and with that came all the sass in the world. Lucy only imagined what trouble her mother had had with her and her many brothers.

"But surely you didn't come to Spruce Valley thinking that Sam was going to pay your way, even if he is a doctor," Josh retorted as he gestured towards Sam. He simply smiled as he bounced Francene on his knee. She giggled happily as she tried to hang on and eat her food at the same time. Lucy scowled at the two of them, which only seemed to egg Sam on.

"No, ye are right, Josh. I didn't expect Sam to pay me way. I was willing to learn how to cook, clean, and do all sorts of housework in order to support Sam as a doctor," Lucy explained. "It wasn't until Martha suggested it that I started the seamstress shop."

"And now the seamstress shop is able to support two other employees," Martha added as she held her son, Samuel, on her lap. Where Francene had grown up into a daring Irish girl, Samuel was often shy and reserved. She guessed that Gray had been the same way as a child.

"I'm sure Emily only did what she has done a hundred times before," Fiona piped in. "I was surprised, since that sort of thing isn't common around here to order so many gowns at once, but I'm sure Lucy and I have made similar purchases in our youth with the intention of our fathers paying for the bill." Josh sighed, appreciating the women's input. However, it only added to his guilt of the way he'd spoken to Emily. He didn't regret speaking honestly with her, but wondered if he could have said things in a better way.

"Seems to me that the ladies should get together and do a

little schooling with Miss Middleton," Gray spoke up further down the table. He was a little busy focusing on eating his food so he could spend the evening with his family as soon as possible, but he felt for Josh. Since Gray was so much older than everyone else, he never thought he'd ever marry. Meeting Martha seemed to be like a dream come true, but it took time to work through her past in order for them to have any future together. And he'd been real hurt when he discovered that Martha had been lying to him during most of their courtship. But in the end, their love for each other had won the battle.

"Hey, that isn't a bad idea," Martha said as she winked at her husband. "Why don't we invite Emily out here to the ranch for a little welcoming party. She'll really get to see what it's like to live in the West when she comes to the ranch." Laughter rang out then as they all knew that it was true.

"I really do like Emily," Fiona said. "And since she was a debutante in Atlanta, she'll enjoy the time to attend a party."

"You always see the best in everyone," Eddie said as he leaned over and kissed his wife on the temple. Fiona giggled and blushed, still getting used to her husband's open way of showing affection to her.

"That is because I know what ugly people look like on the inside," Fiona retorted.

"Then it's settled," Sam spoke up. "We'll have a welcoming party here at the ranch and hopefully help Emily to see what it's like to live in the West."

"And encourage her," Lucy added. "I think she just needs to see her own potential." Josh nodded, thinking that could be the key to the whole situation. Then a smile came to his lips as he thought of something fun they could all do.

"And we should play cards as well," Josh added. "She's been known to play poker." Laughter rang out again. Sawyer, Eddie's brother, shook his head at the idea.

"I'd be willing to see how good she plays," Sawyer spoke up.

"As would I," Eddie agreed with his brother.

"Well, when I go in to open the shop tomorrow, I'll pay Emily a visit and invite her to the party," Fiona said.

"And perhaps we can invite some other women as well," Martha suggested. "Emily needs to see that women can achieve anything they put their minds to. Mayor Stavros would be a welcome addition."

"That's a good idea, Martha," Gray said, always willing to encourage his wife. After all she'd been through, he always wanted to show her that he supported her. They shared a special smile as they looked deeply into each other's eyes.

When the dinner came to an end, Josh stayed and visited with everyone while the dishes were cleaned. Eventually, Gray and Martha left to their own home not too far away from the ranch, along with Eddie and Fiona who had started building their own home. Most of it was done, but the young couple was taking their time with it. Josh was left with the Slaters. And after Sam helped his wife and daughter to bed, he joined Josh in the sitting room.

"How are you feeling about all of this, Josh?" Sam asked as they settled into the chairs by the fire. It hadn't been lit tonight since the weather was warming up, but instead several lanterns hung around the room as the sun set.

"I'm not sure, Sam," Josh admitted with a long sigh. "I

mean, I really am attracted to Emily." Sam chuckled as he nodded.

"Yes, I saw her this morning in passing and noticed that she could easily turn heads," Sam admitted. "But you shouldn't propose just because she's pretty."

"Yeah, Sam, I get that," Josh said, discouraged. "Her letter was just so interesting that I thought for sure she would be the fierce, independent woman I've always been looking for."

"And I'm sure she is, Josh. I mean, she left her home behind to travel here on her own," Sam said. "You do have to give the girl some credit where credit is due." Josh nodded, knowing his friend was right.

"I was just so shocked when Fiona came to me today and gave me that bill. It just drove me nuts," Josh said. "And Bill had mentioned to me after I got Emily settled at the inn that she looked like those type of women that only want a wealthy husband."

"See, now I understand what you've been worried about," Sam said as he pointed at Josh. "You let Bill get in your head." Josh shrugged his shoulders, uncertain if Sam was actually speaking the truth.

"I don't know, Sam. I get this feeling that she thinks working is beneath her and that her husband should do every-thing for her," Josh said honestly.

"And that's probably all she's ever known or expected out of marriage," Sam reasoned. "You'll just have to show her that there's more to life than just money, and that marriage should be founded on love, not some sort of business deal." Josh nodded, knowing that Sam always gave the best advice.

"Well," Josh said as he stood to his feet. "I just hope that this party will do Emily some good. I'd hate to see her so discouraged ever again." Sam stood as well and shook hands with Josh before he left. As Sam watched his best friend leave the ranch house, he said a silent prayer that things would work out between the two.

CHAPTER 9

*B*y the time the next morning came, Emily was feeling all sorts of awful. She hadn't eaten anything since yesterday morning and had been too beside herself with worry to even venture out to get something to eat at The Eatery again. Now, her stomach hurt and she knew she needed to eat something as soon as possible to keep up her strength.

Knowing that no one was going to come to her aid, Emily eventually got out of bed and put on a simple gown. Then, she took the time to braid her hair simply so she didn't need to fuss with it. She figured she could change after she got something in her stomach. She wished she could simply ring a bell and summon a breakfast tray to be brought to her and a bath to be drawn. A quick glance into the looking glass showed that she could really use a good wash of her face, since she looked a bit puffy from crying so much.

Taking a deep breath, Emily made her way from the room

and down the stairs. At the counter was the always present Bill, and when he looked up from his book and saw her current state, his brows furrowed together in concern.

"Are you feeling alright, Miss Middleton?" Bill asked as he set his book down on the counter. Bill noted how she appeared to have been recently upset and wondered if things hadn't gone as planned with the Sheriff.

"Yes, just waited too long to eat something," Emily admitted. "I'm going straightaway to The Eatery now to order something."

"Well, would you like me to go over there for you?" Bill offered. "Perhaps you should rest for a bit." Emily thought about his offer for a moment and decided she would accept his help.

Pulling a few notes from her purse, she handed them to Bill and said, "Thank you so much. Just order whatever Nell suggests. She always has great recommendations."

"Sure, I'll do that for you and bring it on up as soon as it's ready," Bill said as he took the money and pocketed it. He then placed his 'away' sign on the counter before rounding it and heading out.

Emily took her time returning to her room, happy to have accepted Bill's assistance. She left the door unlocked as she entered her room and took a seat at one of the nice wing-backed chairs. Emily could see out the window to the main street below as she watched all sorts of people walking up and down the road. She sighed heavily, her thoughts returning to everything she'd said to Josh, and what he'd said in return.

How could I have been so wrong about the Sheriff? Emily asked herself as she stared almost absentmindedly out the window. She wasn't really focused on who was walking by the inn as much as she wanted to understand how her plan had gone so wrong. Emily had always been perfect at planning and seeing her well thought-out ideas come true. She thought that the Sheriff probably thought she was quite naive and even stupid about what their marriage would look like. And the more she ran their previous conversation through her mind, the more she realized that it was nonetheless true.

When a knock on the door came, Emily called to the person to enter since she assumed that it was Bill returned with some sort of food for her. But as she turned her head and saw that Fiona had just stepped into her room, she was clearly surprised. She instantly felt embarrassed, thinking the woman had come to tell her that she needed to come straightaway to pay for the dresses or have her order canceled. But the closer Emily observed her, the more she thought that she didn't look upset, but perhaps cheerful instead.

"I'm sorry if I'm disturbing you, Miss Middleton," Fiona said, a bit nervous once she realized that Emily looked unwell. Fiona could see the way her cheeks and eyes were puffy, and if she had to guess, she'd say that Emily had been crying.

"No, you're not disturbing me at all. Please, have a seat," Emily said as she motioned to the chair across from her. "You'll have to excuse me though because Bill was kind enough to grab me a bite to eat from The Eatery. It seems I look as bad as I feel." Emily tried to smile, but had a hard time doing so.

"Are you not feeling well?" Fiona asked, wondering if she should go get Dr. Slater.

"Yes, I am well, thank you," Emily reassured her. "I just didn't get much sleep last night and I skipped dinner."

"Oh goodness, you must just feel terrible," Fiona said. She also had the knowledge that she and Josh had shared some unpleasant words but wasn't about to tell Emily that Josh had talked about it with other people. That would probably only make her feel worse.

"Nothing a good meal can't fix," Emily replied.

"Well, I won't keep you long. I simply wanted to come by and personally invite you to a party," Fiona said with a bright smile. The idea of attending a party piqued Emily's interest as she raised an eyebrow at the woman.

"A party? Well, that certainly sounds like a pleasant affair," Emily said.

"Yes, well, when I told the other mail-order-brides of your arrival, they wanted to throw you a welcoming party. So, we want to know if you'll join us tomorrow afternoon at the ranch?" Fiona explained. At first, Emily wanted to agree right away, but then realized that the location didn't sound like it was in town.

"I'd be happy to attend, and I feel honored to have a party thrown for me. But I'm afraid that I'm not sure how I'd get to this ranch," Emily explained. Fiona only smiled brightly as an idea came to mind.

"Well, we've invited quite a few people from town to also attend. I'm sure one of them would like to give you a ride in their wagon," Fiona said, knowing exactly who she was going to ask to do the errand.

"In that case, I have no reason to refuse," Emily said with a genuine smile.

"Fantastic. I'll let the women know you'll be coming tomorrow afternoon," Fiona said as she rose from the chair. "You'll have to excuse me. I must get the shop opened and let everyone know."

"Alright then. Thank you again, Fiona," Emily said as Fiona neared the door.

"Trust me. It's my pleasure," Fiona said with a bright smile before leaving the room. Emily couldn't help but chuckle as Fiona left. She was so enthusiastic that it was almost contagious.

The next time a knock came on the door, Emily was pleased to see Bill coming into her room with a few plates of food on a large wooden serving tray. Emily's eyes grew wide as she saw everything on the tray. Bill had certainly gone out of his way to make sure she was taken care of.

"My goodness, Mr. Eckert. You've certainly outdone yourself," Emily said as she sat forward. Bill began to place the many plates on a nearby table and the aroma started to make Emily's stomach growl with hunger.

"I'm glad you think so," Bill said as he withdrew Emily's change and handed it to her.

"Keep it. I think you deserve it for an outstanding job well done," Emily said with a smile. Bill only nodded as he pocketed the change, pleased to hear Emily's positive words.

"Well, if there is anything else I can help you with, just let me know," Bill said as he neared the door. "When you're done, I can help you take the dishes back over."

"I'll be sure to let you know," Emily said before Bill left the room. Once the door was closed, Emily threw ladylike tendencies out the window. She ate with gusto and enjoyed a little of everything that Bill had brought her. By the time she had finished, not only was most of the food eaten, but she felt rather stuffed to the gills.

With a heavy sigh, Emily set about cleaning up the room and even taking the time to wash her face and hair with the basin of water that resided in the small washroom attached to her room. It was nothing like the indoor plumbing that Emily was used to growing up, but she was starting to realize that it was important for her to count her blessings instead of comparing everything to what she was used to back in Atlanta.

After she'd cleaned up and changed into a gown that was more fitting her stature, she collected all the plates, and when she found the wooden tray in the hallway, she used it to pile up all the plates and take them down the stairs.

"Wow, you really look like you know what you're doing," Bill said as he watched Miss Middleton come down the stairs with the tray balanced perfectly in her hand while the other held up the hem of her dress so she could walk with ease.

"Must have been those years of etiquette training my father put me through," Emily said with a smile as she set the tray down on the counter. "I could probably still walk around with a pile of books balanced on my head." Bill whistled in response as he imagined Miss Middleton doing such a thing.

"Looks like you can also pack it away when you want to," Bill said as he gestured towards all the empty plates. He couldn't fathom how a young lady as slim as Miss Middleton could eat so much.

Emily chuckled as she raised her hand to cover her mouth. "That's what I get for going too long without eating," Emily said. "I'll be more mindful in the future."

"Yes, you do need to take care of yourself," came the Sheriff's voice as he walked into the inn. Emily and Bill immediately went silent as they turned to face Josh as he came towards them. Emily's eyes narrowed at the Sheriff and Bill took that as his cue to give the young couple some privacy. He picked up the tray then and walked out of the inn, intent on returning the plates and giving the two plenty of time to talk.

"Can I help you Sheriff?" Emily asked, not overly keen on the idea of entertaining him at the moment. She was still upset with him and fancied herself a light nap.

"Seems like I can help you, Miss Middleton," Josh said as he came to stop in front of Emily. She looked beautiful in her afternoon gown, and Josh had to remind himself to focus on more than just her good looks. "Fiona told me you need a ride out to the Slater Ranch for the party." Emily inwardly sighed as she thought how Fiona must have asked Josh on purpose.

"Yes, I would appreciate a ride out to the ranch. I think what the women are willing to do for me is very kind and I should have no reason to refuse attending a party," Emily said as she straightened her posture.

"Good. I think you'll enjoy seeing a real ranch and spending time with other people," Josh said with a smirk. His lopsided grin did something to Emily that she couldn't deny. She might be angry at him, but she would never be able to lie about her attraction to him.

"I would agree as well," Emily replied. She then turned away from him, thinking their conversation was done. But Josh quickly caught her hand, pulling Emily to a stop. She was surprised by his bold gesture and she didn't know whether to be angry or flattered.

"I never meant to upset you so much, Emily," Josh said in a soft voice. She stared up into his honey colored eyes, seeming to be lost in them. Her previous thoughts of anger drifted away as she was caught in the moment.

"I understand it wasn't intended," Emily eventually managed to say. He dropped her hand then, needing to get back at the office. He wanted to help the other women in planning this party and didn't want to waste any time since it was planned for the following day.

"Well then, I'll see you tomorrow," Josh said in parting. He tipped his hat to her and finally turned away. Walking out of the inn wasn't a pleasant experience for Josh because he wanted to take the time to discover the real Emily, but figured that only time would tell.

Emily watched Josh walk out of the inn, curious about his motives. She certainly didn't seem to be his ideal wife with her certain ideals of what their marriage would be like, but he seemed to still be making an effort to impress her. Did he expect her to change her way of thinking? Could she really become a working woman and a wife, plus a mother one day? The thoughts alone seemed to exhaust her further as Emily finally made her way back up the stairs and to her room. There, she settled onto the bed with the intent of taking a nap. But the harder she tried to sleep, the more she thought about the handsome sheriff.

CHAPTER 10

*J*osh was looking forward to picking Emily up at the inn that day. After spending so much time the day before helping the Slaters and the others plan for this get-together, he was really looking forward to it himself. That morning he'd dressed in his finest suit, the type he only wore for official business. His goal was to impress Emily and show her that he could still be a gentleman, even if he wasn't very wealthy. And so, Josh made his way over to the inn with the wagon he'd borrowed from the Slaters, because he didn't think Emily would be keen on the idea of riding double on his mare.

After he pulled the wagon to a stop in front of the inn, Josh took a deep breath. He really hoped that Emily would enjoy herself today, but also see what living in the West was all about. He hoped that Emily would see from the other women what it took to be successful in this town, and not just the work they did. Emily would have to learn to cook and clean for herself, along with all the other chores that must be completed by hand. If anything, Josh hoped that Emily would see how satisfying it was to do things for yourself and gain that feeling of self-accomplishment. Perhaps she'd never felt like that before and would soon see that spark of life in the other women today.

Josh entered the inn, thinking about the way he'd reached out and touched Emily the day before. It had been his gut instinct that propelled him to take that action. He'd come to the inn the day before after talking to Fiona, but a part of him really wanted Emily to know that he hadn't given up on her, even if they'd had a disagreement. He knew he'd been a little rough with Emily when it came to his word choice, and now he'd hoped to *show* Emily what he meant, more than just tell her.

Josh dipped his head to Bill at the counter, who sitting and reading a novel. Bill didn't seem to pay him any attention as Josh took the stairs to the rooms upstairs. When he reached Emily's door, he quickly knocked and waited for her to answer. When the door opened, Josh's mouth fell open. Emily had done her hair up, her black hair framing her face in ringlets. She wore a simple gown, one that he'd figured would be used for working that day. It wasn't at all fancy, but she still was as beautiful as ever.

"I picked it up from Frost's yesterday evening when I stopped by for dinner," Emily said as she watched Josh's eyes roam over her from head to toe. She hadn't expected this type of reaction from him because she considered the dress to be rather plain. But it appeared as if Josh approved. "I was surprised that they had in stock a gown already made that fit me, but I figured that it would be good for going out to the ranch."

Josh smiled at her, feeling proud of her for what she'd done. He figured that she felt like it was below her to purchase a premade gown and one so simple. But the fact that she'd done it and actually thought ahead proved to Josh that Emily had the ability to not only think for herself, but think logically enough about situations and the best way to go about them. It was the instinct needed not only in his profession, but also living a long and successful life in the West.

"I think you look lovely," Josh said as their eyes met. "Though, I think you'd make a burlap sack look good." Emily couldn't contain her laughter as she imagined herself only dressed in a sack. She didn't even have time to cover her mouth as she laughed, hugging her middle. Josh thought she was even more beautiful as she laughed freely.

"My goodness, I hope we never have to put that thought to the test," Emily said as her mirth subsided. "But I appreciate the compliment." Emily stepped out of her room and locked the door, placing the key in her purse. She then accepted Josh's arm as he offered it to her and he led her down the stairs. In the lobby they waved to Bill, who still seemed to be too engrossed in his novel to notice them. Little did they know that Bill was simply giving them privacy and as many moments alone as possible. He really did hope that the Sheriff would fall in love, and even though Emily was good looking, that perhaps she'd also show how she could be a good wife, too.

Outside of the inn, Josh helped Emily up into the wagon. She'd never ridden in such a thing before, having always had the pleasure of riding in an elegant carriage. Even the stage-coach had been finely constructed for its fast travels yet comfortable seating for riders. But the wagon was simply made, and the front bench was rather uncomfortable. Emily only hoped that it wouldn't be very far outside of town to the Slater's ranch.

Josh pulled himself up into the driver's seat and quickly took the reins. With a flick of his wrist, he sent his mare into a canter. Emily held firmly to the side of the wagon, not used to the sudden momentum of such a thing. But as they traveled out of town, she got used to the rhythm and eventually loosened her death grip on the wagon.

"Would you like to try driving the wagon?" Josh asked as he closed the distance between them, scooching over on the sitting board and handing the reins to her. Emily was surprised by the offer, never having considered driving herself. She'd always had a driver to take care of that business, but knew she couldn't turn down the offer. She was curious about driving and figured it couldn't hurt.

Emily took the reins in her hands and felt a sudden jolt of fear run through her. What if she did it wrong? What if she got them hurt?

"Easy now," Josh said, his soft voice seeming to pierce through her mind. "Loosen up your grip. She'll know if you're nervous."

"She?" Emily asked, her eyes focused only on the road. She tried to loosen her hands around the leather reins while taking a few deep breaths.

"Yes, Emily," Josh said with a chuckle. "The horse is a mare." Emily's eyes moved to the horse for a second, thinking she'd never really paid much attention to the gender of horses before.

"Alright, now what do I do?" Emily asked.

"Well, you'll want to put some slack in the reins if you want her to pick up her pace. You only tighten them when you want her to slow down or come to a full stop," Josh instructed as he placed his hands around hers. He moved his fingers till slack was applied to the reins, letting the mare know she had more range of motion and could pick up her speed. Soon she moved from a canter to a trot, and then a full gallop. Emily couldn't contain her smile as she listened to the wheels of the wagon thundering down the road, mixed with the sound of the mare's hooves and the feel of the wind whipping by her face. She'd never done anything like this before and found it to be exhilarating.

Josh kept his hands on Emily's so he could help her steer the wagon around the rutted part of the roads. He was enjoying this experience with her. And though he was certain she could figure it all out on her own, he liked the excuse to keep his hands around hers. As he looked down at her, the wagon rolling down the road at a steady pace, he was pleased to see how happy she looked and even excited about such a mundane thing. Josh often took horseback riding for granted since it was the fast way to travel around Spruce Valley. But by the look on Emily's face, he had a solid guess that she would find it very enjoyable and almost thrilling. He smirked, thinking of the idea of horse racing with her one day.

Before too long, they made their way to the Slater's ranch. Emily had enjoyed the thrill of driving the wagon mixed with the beautiful scenery that passed them by. The land seemed to go on forever with only the horizon coming to meet it. Small houses dotted the landscape with various amounts of cattle and sheep grazing in the distance. Emily had never seen livestock before and found them very interesting.

As they came upon the ranch, Josh helped Emily pull on the reins, causing his mare to slow. After growing up in a city, the vast expanse of farmland that spread out before them was a surprise to Emily. She'd gotten glimpses of fields and forests on the trip to Spruce Valley, but she hadn't yet seen a ranch. A sea of prairie grass stretched out as far as Emily could see, meeting the dazzling blue sky above the horizon. Maple and birch trees dotted the ranch and there was a white bunkhouse on the left of the driveway.

A small one-story, white clapboard ranch house stood a little way down the lane on the right. A large red barn had been erected farther down the lane with wooden fencing running out from the back of it. Several heads of cattle grazed in the pasture and Emily found them fascinating, if not strange smelling. Emily looked at it all, finding it quite charming and welcoming. There was a large wraparound porch on the ranch house and based on the size, she figured it would be rather roomy on the inside. She had figured that ranch homes were nothing more than a shack, but this structure completely proved her wrong.

The front door opened, and several women came out quickly to greet her. Emily recognized Fiona and assumed the other two to be the other ladies that worked at the seamstress shop. The short, black haired one had a very large belly, so she assumed that had to be Mrs. Slater, and therefore the other must be Martha Jenkins.

"Welcome, Emily!" Fiona called from the front porch as Josh came around and helped her down from the wagon. Emily couldn't deny that she enjoyed the feeling of Josh's strong hands on her waist as he helped her down. She tried not to show how much she enjoyed the feeling and instead focused her attention on the three women smiling down at her from the porch.

"Hello ladies. It's good to see you again, Fiona, and a pleasure to make all of your acquaintances," Emily said as she joined them on the porch.

"It is a pleasure to meet ye as well, Emily," Lucy said. "Please, come in."

"I'll be right in after I get the wagon put away," Josh called after Emily. She waved at him before following the women inside the ranch house. As predicted, Emily was pleasantly surprised by the lovely ranch house. The majority of the front room housed a large dining room with a decent sized sitting room to the left. Towards the back was a wide and open kitchen where she could smell all sorts of pleasant aromas coming to meet her. She could spot a long hallway to one side and figured that was where all the bedrooms where located.

Two small children ran towards her, seeming to chase after one another as they zoomed through the house. But when they saw that there was someone new in the house, they came to a full stop in front of her, their wide eyes looking up at her with curiosity.

"Francene, Samuel, I'd like you to meet Miss Emily Middleton," Martha introduced. "The party we've put together is for her."

The young girl placed her hands on her hips as she looked

up at Emily. "Is it your birthday today?" Francene asked in her very young voice.

"No, it is not," Emily answered with a smile. "But sometimes it's fun to simply have a party for the sake of celebrating." Francene seemed pleased with her response as she resumed a game of tag around the house with little Samuel. They both seemed to be about two years old and full of laughter and light.

"What lovely children," Emily observed as the ladies watched the little ones play.

"They are the joy of me life," Lucy spoke up as she rubbed her stomach. Emily remembered how Fiona had explained that Lucy was meant to be on bed rest till her next child was born. She hoped that she wasn't putting any extra stress on the woman. "Well, let me give ye the tour of our grand house."

Together, the women showed Emily all the different parts of the ranch house. Emily found the house to be warm and inviting. Everything had a purpose, and even though they were practically in the middle of nowhere, Emily found that the house had many modern features such as a water closet and an ice chest.

"Eddie and I are still building our house, but we hope to put in a water closet as well," Fiona said as she saw how Emily marveled at it. "After staying with the Slaters last year when I arrived in Spruce Valley, I was certain I'd never be able to live without one."

"I'm sure it is very difficult to get running water away from town," Emily observed.

"As long as one can access running water below ground, there can then be enough pressure added to the pipes to draw it up," Martha explained. "The home Gray and I built was completely finished when we were able to tap into underground water. My goodness, that was a terrible mess at first." They all laughed at the story and Emily realized how much she missed being with other ladies. There was a need to socialize inside of Emily that she hadn't really satisfied since arriving at Spruce Valley.

"Well, me dears. It seems I've reached my limit," Lucy said as she wrapped her arms around her belly. "I'm going to go lay down for a wee bit and see if I can stitch a gown together."

"Sounds good, Lucy," Fiona said. "We'll make sure to keep an eye on Francene."

"Much obliged," Lucy called back as she waddled down the hallway to what Emily assumed was the main bedroom.

"Speaking of, we should probably get lunch on the table," Martha spoke up, the sound of the children laughing coming from the sitting room.

"What do you normally like to eat?" Fiona asked Emily as they walked back into the main part of the house.

"Oh, I'm not very picky," Emily assured them. "Anything would be lovely."

"Well, let's try our hand at Johnnycakes with some pork and Mormon gravy," Martha said with an eager voice. Emily had never heard of this type of food before but was at least willing to watch. But as soon as the women entered the kitchen portion of the house, Emily was soon enlisted to help out with preparing the meal. Though Emily didn't really feel confident about what she was doing, she was at least happy to have thorough instructions and happy company.

By the time they'd finished the meal, Josh had joined them in the house. He couldn't contain his large grin as he looked at Emily. She was now in an apron and had flour all over her. It was his chuckle that told Emily he'd come into the house. When she looked at him, she gave him a devilish grin that seemed to stop his laughter cold in his tracks. He simply shook his head then as he left to go play with the children in the sitting room. They were all playing blocks and the children would laugh loudly any time Josh would knock over the blocks, pretending to be a burglar. Emily watched him play with the children for a moment, thinking that he'd really make a great father.

When the food was served to the table, Emily put up her apron and joined them. She had to admit that she felt a feeling of accomplishment as she looked at all the food she'd helped make. Even though it was purely based on Martha and Fiona's guidance, she could at least feel proud of helping out. And as she tried everything, she was surprised at how delicious it all tasted.

"Good job, Emily," Samuel spoke up after he'd eaten everything off his plate. She was surprised by the compliment and smiled happily at the young boy.

"Why thank you, Samuel," she replied. Josh was watching her the whole time, thinking he hadn't seen her smile this much since arriving in Spruce Valley. He was happy to see her doing so well on the ranch and was excited to teach her a few things himself.

After they all helped clean up the dishes, Fiona took a plate of food to Lucy while Martha put the children down for their afternoon nap, despite their much protesting. Emily couldn't help but smile as she watched them go down the hallway to the nursery. She hadn't spent much time around children and thought they were utterly adorable.

When Josh took her hand, she almost jumped because she was so focused on everything around her. He smiled at her and tugged her from the house. When they stepped onto the front porch, Emily asked, "Where are we going now?"

"I figured you'd like to see the rest of the ranch and perhaps try your luck at riding a horse," Josh explained as he led her by the hand towards the barn.

"Riding a horse?" Emily questioned, surprised. "Don't you think that learning to drive a wagon is enough for one day?" She was nervous about the idea of riding a horse, but never really liked to back down from a challenge or show fear or weakness. That wasn't her nature because she always enjoyed impressing others, so she did her best to control her nerves as she allowed Josh to lead her into the barn.

"The only way you'll learn to survive in the West is by learning these basic skills as soon as you can," Josh explained. "I know you're an independent woman, Emily. I just want you to continue being so here in Spruce Valley." Emily was certainly touched by his words and figured she'd give it her best shot.

"Alright, so I have my mare saddled and ready for you," Josh explained as he let go of Emily's hand and went into the stable to bring his mare out. "I'll follow behind you on one of Sam's extra horses he keeps just in case. The horse should need the extra exercise anyways." Emily could only watch in wonder as Josh led the mare out to her. She tried not to be nervous as she reached out her hand and let her fingers brush against the horse's neck. She found the horsehair to be rather soft and soon enjoyed the feeling of petting the horse. The mare seemed to enjoy it as well as she pushed against Emily's fingers.

"I think she likes me," Emily said as she looked at Josh. She saw how close he was watching her and only hoped that she was making a good impression on him.

"Of course, she does," Josh said as he motioned Emily over to him. "Now, I want you to put your foot into the stirrups here and push up with all your might until you can get your other leg on the other side."

"But won't my legs show if I do that?" Emily asked, thinking that it would be rather risky to be seen in such a position.

"Your calves might show a bit, yes. But you can draw your knees up and together if you're worried about it," Josh explained. "Trust me. No one would dare look at your calves while you're with me." When he winked at her, she couldn't help but blush. Taking a deep breath, she tried to focus on the task at hand. She approached the mare and placed her foot into the stirrup while reaching up and grabbing the saddle horn. When she counted to three, she pushed up with all her might as Josh guided her up onto the saddle with his hands. Again, the feeling of his strong hands on her sent a wave of warmth through her. Emily did her best to shake it off as she placed her other foot in the stirrup and gripped onto the saddle horn as she tried to find her balance. Though the hem of her gown had risen, it wasn't too much and she thought she'd be able to ride without worrying about her gown too much.

"You look like a natural," Josh said with a chuckle. Emily shook her head, knowing that he was teasing her.

"Nice try," Emily replied as she brought up her knees a bit against the mare, feeling more secure by doing so. She then took the reins, her hips gripping the saddle as she tried not to think too much about falling off.

"Alright, just hold on one second and then we'll head out," Josh said as he quickly mounted the other horse and then guided it towards Emily. "Now, it's just like driving the wagon. More slack will tell the horse to go faster while a tight grip will keep the horse going slow." Emily just nodded as she watched Josh lead his horse out of the barn. She took one more deep breath before she rubbed her heels against the mare's sides, urging the horse forward. She tried not to pull on the reins too tightly as the mare followed after Josh's horse, seeming to know what to do.

Once they were in the pasture, Josh set his horse to a canter. Emily did her best to mimic the action, letting the reins loosen in her hands. As the mare began to canter, Emily found that she had to focus more on her balance. She did her best to move her body with the movements of the horse, which were quite jarring experiencing them for the first time. But eventually Emily got used to the quickened speed of the horse.

As soon as Emily seemed to be getting comfortable, Josh would increase their pace. He wanted to push Emily to show her that she was full of potential and really could do more than she ever thought possible. He could see the fire and determination in her eyes, close to the same fierceness he witnessed in the photo she'd sent him and also in the words she used when she'd written her letter. Josh was eager to show Emily that she had a strength deep inside her that she could avail herself to at any given time. She'd already proven herself brave by traveling all the way to Spruce Valley on her own, and now he wanted her to see that same strength for herself.

Before too long, their horses were galloping through the empty pasture. Emily smiled brightly as the wind whipped by her, the feeling of the strong horse beneath her as the hooves thundered across the grass in quick rhythm. Emily could hardly believe that she was riding a horse as they raced around the pasture. Dust flew up behind them, and Emily had never felt so free in her life. She was in complete control and she wanted this feeling to be never-ending.

After a time, Josh slowed his horse, indicating for Emily to do so as well. She figured that the horses could use a break after they'd put them through their paces. The two horses then trotted side by side as Emily did her best to catch her breath.

"So, what do you think of riding a horse now?" Josh asked, his lopsided grin having returned to his face. He looked at her with a satisfied expression and Emily couldn't help but chuckle.

"I think it's the most wonderful thing in the world," Emily said as she reached down and patted the mare's neck once more. The mare nickered in return, seeming to enjoy all the special attention.

"I knew you would enjoy it. If you enjoy poker, then I knew you'd enjoy something as thrilling as riding a horse," Josh said. Emily shook her head, wondering if it had been wrong of her to tell Josh that little detail.

"I do find riding a horse thrilling, but it's more of a sense of freedom and control that I enjoyed the most," Emily explained. "It's something I never really felt before."

"Well, you're in Spruce Valley now with all sorts of opportunities and possibilities ahead of you," Josh said, trying to be encouraging.

"I guess I need to experience these opportunities before I can appreciate any of it," Emily admitted. "Much like being shown how to ride a horse and learning that it's quite enjoyable."

"As long as you're willing, I'm sure you could accomplish anything you put your mind to," Josh said, his voice growing soft. They shared a particular look and a part of Emily wanted to say something in relation to marriage. But she figured that now wasn't the best time for that. It seemed that Emily first had to learn to get her feet under her before she could really start thinking about marriage with a guy like Josh. He had some pretty high expectations that she wasn't sure she could fulfill at this time.

The sound of whooping voices brought Emily's attention back to the front of the ranch house. Her eyes grew large as she saw a small group of Indians approaching. Her first instinct was to gallop away on the horse in fear of an attack, but when she saw Martha and Fiona come onto the porch with scowling faces, Emily only grew more confused.

"That is Bright Star and his sons," Josh explained. "I bet Martha is giving them a good tongue lashing for being so loud when the children are sleeping." Emily still watched the scene with wide eyes while Josh simply chuckled. "Come on. I'll introduce you."

"But aren't Indians dangerous?" Emily quickly asked, uncertain about getting close to them.

"Yes, Emily, Indians can be dangerous. Just like a wild bear can be dangerous when provoked," Josh explained. "The local Crow Tribe is very friendly to everyone in Spruce Valley. Dr. Slater even employs a few to watch over his sheep further down the road." Emily was finding this all rather bazaar but was willing to meet them if Josh assured her that she would be safe. Slowly but surely, they led the horses out of the pasture and back into the barn. And once the horses had been released of their saddles and brushed down, something Emily really enjoyed doing, Josh then took her hand once more and led her towards the house to meet Indians for the first time.

CHAPTER 11

*E*mily tightened her grip on Josh's hand as he led her from the barn towards the front of the house where the women were visiting with the Indians as though they were old friends. She watched as the older Indian laughed loudly, finding something rather funny. They seemed so normal that Emily almost forgot that the three men were Indians. They were dressed in deerskin trousers, but their chests were bare, save from the long necklaces they wore. Emily had never seen a man so exposed before and did her best not to look at their bodies.

"Oh good, the Sheriff is here," Martha spoke up as they came near. "Now he'll have to order you to wear some clothing when you come to the ranch."

"I think the next time I come to visit, me and my sons shall only wear our breechcloths and have your husbands wear them, too. Then you won't complain so much," Bright Star replied, causing them all to laugh at the idea while Emily only watched with much curiosity. Eventually, she made eye contact with the older Indian and had a hard time looking away.

"Bright Star, may I introduce you to Miss Emily Middleton," Josh spoke up as he watched the exchange between the two. "She has just come in from the East."

"Ah, it is nice to meet you, Emily Middleton," Bright Star said. "I am pleased that you are here for the Sheriff. If he is married soon, then perhaps he won't be so grumpy all the time." Emily couldn't contain her smile then and Bright Star felt pleased to have caused the newcomer to smile. He could tell by the way she looked at him that she'd never seen an Indian before.

"Come now, Bright Star. I am not a grumpy person," Josh said in his defense.

"You forget, Josh Ryder. I did travel with you for many days. I know how you are in the morning," Bright Star retorted, causing Emily to chuckle this time. She was enjoying watching this banter between the two. Josh scowled at the Indian then, even though there was a smile on his face.

"And if Josh doesn't prove himself worthy of such a beautiful creature," Bright Star continued as he focused his gaze on Emily, "I have two sons that are eligible." Running Bear and Sky Bird, Bright Star's sons, both rolled their eyes while remaining silent. Emily had a feeling that Bright Star liked to tease everyone, including his sons.

"Then I shall have to remind Josh often that I have other suitors to consider," Emily teased back, another round of laughter rising into the air.

"I think I will very much enjoy your company, Emily

Middleton. I am glad you are here now," Bright Star said, a twinkle in his eye.

"The feeling is mutual, I assure you," Emily said with a smile. But that smile was quickly wiped off her face as she witnessed a small furry thing race across the grass to climb up onto Bright Star's shoulder. She stared at the animal as it screeched at Bright Star, completely in shock. It took her a second to realize that the animal was in fact a monkey.

"Why hell, Jack," Bright Star said in a fond voice as he took the monkey from his shoulder and cradled it in his arms. "How are you doing today?" The monkey seemed to chatter back at him and continued to do so until Bright Star gave the monkey a date. Satisfied, he relaxed into the Indian's arms like a baby.

"I'm guessing you've never seen a monkey before," Fiona spoke up as she watched Emily's surprised expression, finding it rather humorous.

"Not this close before, no," Emily said. "There was a circus I once went to, but all the animals were in cages." Bright Star scowled at hearing Emily's words.

"That is very unfortunate," Bright Star said as he petted the monkey.

"I won Jack in a poker game," came the voice of a man. Emily turned to see several men having rode in from the pasture and were now making their way to the ranch house. The one that had spoken was a bit taller than Emily with very broad shoulders. He had light brown hair and dark colored eyes.

"Emily, may I introduce you to my husband, Eddie Sawyer," Fiona said as she went to her husband and wrapped her arms around him. Such signs of affection were new to Emily, and realizing she still held Josh's hand, she quickly let it go and folded her hands together in front of her. Josh noticed what she'd done but didn't mind at all. Emily might have come to Spruce Valley with designs to marry him, but he wasn't going to put any pressure on her.

"It's a pleasure to meet you, Eddie," Emily replied. "I didn't think people kept monkeys for pets."

"And I never knew a woman who played poker," Eddie said with a wink. Emily pretended to be surprised as she glared at Josh. He simply raised his hands and took a step back, much to the amusement of everyone.

"Well, I'd be glad to show you just how well I play poker anytime you wish," Emily said to Eddie. "But you may keep your monkey when you lose." This really tickled everyone's funny bone and eventually, Martha called everyone inside for a light snack before dinner was done. Josh couldn't help but be proud of the way Emily had stood up for herself. He could tell that she was finally coming out of her shell and showing everyone her true character.

Emily ended up meeting all sorts of people. Gray, the foreman, and Martha's husband, was introduced to her. She found him to be a very intimidating man, but when the children woke from their nap, she saw that he had a soft side to him as he played with the children in the sitting room. Emily also met the other two ranch hands. Sawyer, who was Eddie's brother, and Tom Barker, one of Sam's original ranch hands. Eventually the good doctor joined all those that had gathered when he returned to the ranch later in the afternoon after closing the clinic a bit early in town.

Emily enjoyed putting in a helping hand with finishing up the rest of dinner. She was surprised to learn that most meals happened in this way as Lucy had been cooking for everyone on the ranch since she came to Spruce Valley. She couldn't imagine cooking for so many people every day and had to give the women a lot of credit. They not only cooked and cleaned while raising children, but also managed a small business in town. Lucy eventually joined the group and sat at the head of the table after showing off the beautiful gown she'd finished while she had been resting in bed. Emily could tell that the woman was very determined, but also mindful of how her body was reacting to this pregnancy. Josh eventually told Emily the deal the two had made that Lucy would listen to her husband's instructions if Josh was willing to share gossip with her when he came out to the ranch from town.

"I never thought a Sheriff would ever admit to being a gossip," Emily said in the hopes of teasing him.

"And I never thought a beautiful debutante would ever ride a horse as well as you have," Josh quickly replied with a wink. Emily couldn't contain her mirth, thinking that Josh would be a good contender for her witty remarks.

As the sun set, candles were lit all around the ranch house. Everyone settled down at the table for dinner, including the Indians. Emily never thought that she'd be sharing a meal with Indians present, but was finding their company rather amusing. Bright Star's sons seemed to relax after a while and proved to be as witty as his father. Another thing that surprised Emily was how delicious all the food was. The shepherd's pie with homemade apple sauce and bread were absolutely delicious and she could imagine herself trying her hand at the dishes once again.

When dinner was through, Martha and Gray took their son home while Lucy went to bed with Francene. That left Fiona and Emily as the only women present when everyone settled down at the table to play poker.

"It's been a while since I've played this game," Bright Star said as Eddie started to pass out the cards for the first round. "I'm not sure if I remember how to do so."

Sawyer, who had been rather quiet during dinner, spoke up and said, "Don't believe a thing this Indian says." Emily chuckled as the two shared a particular look. Emily enjoyed playing poker because it often showed a person's true nature. People who were mostly charming and nice could turn mean and nasty when they started to lose. But tonight, they were only playing for toothpicks so hopefully there wouldn't be so much tension.

Emily quickly learned that her original idea was wrong as she saw how competitive everyone became as the game progressed. Emily and Fiona often laughed together as they watched the men quickly raise bids just to see if they could prove something. It wasn't long before one by one, the men started to lose all their toothpicks while Fiona and Emily's piles continued to grow larger and larger.

"How is it that you two have all the toothpicks," Josh said at one point, gesturing to the women.

"That is because women have more patience than men," Emily reasoned.

"And you all make it so easy," Fiona added, causing everyone to laugh.

After a while, it was only Emily, Josh, and Eddie left playing cards. Even Fiona had lost all she had when she thought she'd had a great running but lost it all in the end. Emily was determined to win and was keeping a very close eye on her competitors. The other two seemed to be sizing her up as well and Emily did her best to keep her breathing steady and not to give away any signs of what cards she held in her hands. But eventually, she started to bid them up, feeling like she'd finally gotten a spread of cards that could win her the game.

With all three of their toothpicks in the middle of the table, everyone watched and waited for the remaining players to start laying down their cards. Everyone was dying to see if Emily would be able to beat the two men, and as Josh and Eddie laid down their cards, both with straights, Emily did her best to contain her glee.

"Read 'em and weep, boys," Emily said as she laid down her cards, showing that she had a flush. It took a second for everyone to realize that Emily had won, and before they could raise a fuss, Dr. Slater was quick to shush them all.

"Remember, Lucy and Francene are sleeping," Sam said, his serious eyes meeting everyone else's. They all covered their mouths till their mirth had subsided. Emily didn't even bother grabbing all the toothpicks from the middle of the table as she simply laughed with the others.

"My goodness. I should really be heading back to town now," Emily said as she helped clean up the toothpicks and all the cards.

"I'll take you back to town then," Josh said as he stood from the table with Emily.

"Miss Middleton. Why don't you consider coming to stay with Lucy and I till you can get on your feet?" Dr. Slater offered. "We have a spare bedroom that isn't currently being used." Emily was surprised by the offer. She glanced at Josh, wondering what he thought of the plan. She didn't really like the idea of being so far from town, and Josh, but knew that she couldn't afford to stay at the inn forever.

"I'd be happy to accept that offer, Dr. Slater. I don't have many skills, but I'd be willing to offer my help in return," Emily said.

"I'm sure Lucy will appreciate hearing that," Dr. Slater agreed.

"Then we shall come once again to play poker with you, Emily Middleton. This was very enjoyable," Bright Star said as he rose from the table with his sons. Without another word, they slipped from the house almost soundlessly, showing Emily just how skillful the Indians were.

"Well then, we shall see you all tomorrow. I'll bring Emily back out with her things then," Josh said. "Good night everyone." Emily took the time to say goodnight and to thank them for such a wonderful day. Then, she followed Josh out of the house and into the night air. It was cool and refreshing since Emily had grown quite warm during the poker game. But she was pleased with herself for having played another good game of poker and left with more friends than she felt she ever had.

Emily accompanied Josh as they got the wagon ready to head back into town. Though it was dark, the moon shed enough light on the Earth to allow them to see what they were doing. And by the time they were done and ready to head out, Emily couldn't deny that she felt a little proud of the small accomplishment. There were so many new things that she'd learned to do in one day that it was a bit overwhelming to process. She let Josh help her up into the wagon. This time, as Josh drove them into town, he kept the reins to himself, allowing Emily to simply relax and enjoy the ride back to town.

The world seemed to be cast into a soft glow of the moon, giving the scenery a mystical appearance. Thousands of stars shone from above and Emily took a minute to watch them. She was grateful for the day she'd had on the Slater's ranch, simply learning new skills and enjoying the company of others. She felt more satisfied than she had in months and thought for a moment that she could really learn to love Spruce Valley.

Even though Josh knew he needed to keep his eyes alert for danger, especially since they were traveling by night, he couldn't help but watch Emily from time to time as her eyes drifted towards the heavens. He was immensely proud of Emily and all that she'd accomplished today. He felt like she could really fit into the community of Spruce Valley and find her own way. He wasn't certain how she felt about him or whether or not they had a shot at marriage, but he was willing to be patient and continue to watch Emily bloom and prosper in her new environment. He didn't particularly like the idea of Emily staying so far away from town but was certain that Lucy could use the extra help around the house since she was bedridden. Josh knew that Lucy had become quite restless at home since Martha took the kids into town with her during the day. And having another lady in the house would surely do Lucy as much good as Emily.

By the time they reached town, Josh was almost sad that their time together had finally come to an end. He stopped the wagon in front of the inn and went to hop down to help Emily from the wagon, when she reached out and touched his shoulder, stopping him.

"I just wanted to say thank you for everything today," Emily said, her hand still resting on his shoulder. He smiled at her and nodded.

"It was nothing," Josh replied.

"Fiona told me how it was your idea," Emily admitted with a smirk on her lips. Josh chuckled, thinking he'd want to throttle Fiona right now for letting that detail slip. But he was certain the woman was only trying to be helpful.

"Well, it was really the women that made it happen. I only made sure everyone knew about it. Mayor Stavros unfortunately couldn't make it to the get together tonight, but promises to make it up to you," Josh explained.

"I'm sure I will get to meet her soon enough," Emily assured him. "It's a small town after all." Josh nodded, certain of her words. He then finally got down from the wagon and then helped Emily down before walking with her to the front door of the inn.

"I also wanted to apologize," Emily spoke up, trying to muster up all her courage. "It was wrong of me to assume so much of you in relation to my ideals of marriage." Josh had assumed that they'd visit this topic of conversation once more and figured now was as good as any time to discuss it.

"I think people often have the wrong idea of what marriage is supposed to be like," Josh said, trying to be reassuring. "It's why people who are married say that it takes hard work from both people to make a marriage successful." Emily simply nodded, hoping that Josh accepted her apology. He surprised her then as he neared her and lowered his lips to hers. Emily had never really been kissed before because she didn't want people to be able to gossip about her in that way. She was surprised by how warm Josh's lips were and returned the kiss with eagerness. But as quickly as the kiss started, it soon ended, leaving Emily wanting more.

"I hope you don't mind me being so forward," Josh said in a husky voice, his words sending shivers all over Emily's body.

"No, I don't mind," Emily replied as her chest rose and fell with excitement. "It's good to know if we are compatible in that way."

"And do you think we are?" Josh asked, his lopsided grin showing once more.

"I feel like I do have a pretty good idea," Emily agreed. "Goodnight, Josh." Emily turned the handle of the door and pushed it open.

"Goodnight, Emily," Josh replied as he took a step away from the inn, tempted to follow Emily to bed. But he didn't want to treat Emily like other women of his past. He wanted to treat her like a real lady.

When Emily shut the door, Josh got back into the wagon and made quick work of getting over to the livery stables to put away his mare and store the wagon. He knew that tomorrow he'd return the wagon to the ranch, along with Emily and all her things. He was grateful for his friend offering to house Emily, and it was turning into a mail-order-bride tradition. He was certain that Emily would enjoy being out on the ranch even if it seemed to put distance between them.

When Emily got to her room, she locked the door behind her and began to get ready for bed. She couldn't believe how wonderful her day had been and a part of her was looking forward to returning to the ranch. It was so peaceful out there and she'd really enjoyed herself. And though she'd have to rely on Josh coming out to the ranch to visit with her, she was certain that peaceful scenery would really help her to feel relaxed in Spruce Valley. She wanted to find her place in the community and figured that she could spend this time discovering what she wanted to do with the rest of her life.

Just like riding a horse for the first time, Emily suddenly felt this huge sense of freedom she hadn't really felt before. Though her father had been very lenient of Emily in Atlanta, she'd always adhered to society's rules of how she should act and dress.. But now that she was in Spruce Valley, she seemed to be able to act however she felt. To a certain degree, of course. But here in this small Montana town she felt she could become whomever she wanted to. Or perhaps the young lady she'd always dreamed of one day becoming.

CHAPTER 12

*A*fter about a week out at the Slater's ranch, Emily was finally starting to get a hang of things. While Lucy rested in bed or in a chair, she gave Emily instructions on how to do the simplest of things. Whether that was cooking or washing her own laundry, Lucy was there to make sure that Emily knew what she was doing. And now, after doing so for a few days, Emily thought she was finally starting to learn a few things instead of constantly burning the food or not cooking it well enough. Thankfully, everyone had been supportive of Emily as she continued to learn and never said anything that would put her down.

One particular afternoon Josh rode out to the ranch, hoping to steal Emily away from the ranch house for a bit to enjoy a ride into the countryside. He hadn't seen Emily since he'd dropped her and the wagon off at the ranch. After a whole week, Josh was eager to spend some time with Emily again and to learn for himself how she'd been doing at the ranch. As he came down the lane and saw her pinning wet clothes on the line, he smiled brightly. After the conversation they'd had about Emily never working a day in her life, he was pleasantly surprised to see her doing such housework.

"Well, hello there, pretty lady," Josh said as he rode his mare over to where she was in the yard. "I don't suppose you can tell me where I can find Miss Middleton, a debutante from the famous city of Atlanta?" Emily chuckled at Josh's teasing as she finished hanging up a gown before turning her attention to the Sheriff.

"I'm afraid the Miss Middleton of Atlanta no longer exists, and instead you'll just have to visit with Emily," she replied with a happy grin on her face.

"Well, I think I'd like that very much," Josh replied. She was so happy to see him that for a moment they simply stared into one another's eyes. But after a little while, Emily became conscious of herself once more and soon invited him for a bite to eat.

"Actually, I was hoping you wouldn't mind joining me for a ride?" Josh said. Emily was excited about the idea as she looked down at the basket of washed clothes she still needed to hang up.

"If you'll help me hang the wash, I'm sure Lucy won't mind me being away from the house for a bit," Emily suggested.

"I guess I can help out," Josh said in a mocked voice as he climbed down from his mare and began to help Emily clip up all the wet laundry to dry on the beautiful spring day. The moment they were done, Emily went inside to hang up her damp apron and let Lucy know where she was going.

"Ye two have fun," Lucy called after her as Emily left, thinking the woman would want to know all the details when she returned. Josh hadn't minced his words when he said that Lucy liked to gossip. She herself didn't mind doing so as well and spent most of their time talking while they worked.

Back outside, Emily joined Josh by his mare. "Are you going to go saddle up another horse?" Emily asked.

"I thought you wouldn't mind riding double with me," Josh said. "I'll have you ride in front." Emily thought it was rather forward, but as she remembered their kiss, she thought that she'd like to be a bit more daring with Josh. She could tell that they had a mutual attraction to one another, but marriage was much more than just that.

"Just help me up and I'm sure we'll make do," Emily replied. Josh smiled as he helped Emily up into the saddle, loving the feeling of her in his hands, and once he was in the saddle behind her, he did his best to keep his mind clear instead of muddled with different thoughts.

With the reins in his hands and Emily's on the saddle horn, Josh steered the mare for the open countryside and took off at a trot before going into a full gallop. Emily smiled brightly, loving the feeling of riding a horse and traveling quickly across the land on such a strong animal. Her joy was increased with the feeling of Josh right behind her. With all the work she'd been doing the past week, it was surely nice to take a break from it all and simply enjoy the day.

After a while, Josh pulled on the reins and brought the mare to a stop. He slid down from the saddle and then helped Emily down before leading her to a tree where they could get out of the sun for a bit. They settled under the tree and Josh made sure to give Emily plenty of space as they sat and watched the clouds pass by. His mare grazed on the grass and Josh placed his full attention on Emily, thinking she'd really progressed since she first arrived in Spruce Valley.

"You know, Josh. I really do think you'd make a good marshal," Emily spoke up at one point. Josh was surprised to hear this and was worried she was going to start pressuring him again. "You are so kind and helpful, Josh, that it makes me wonder what kind of good you'd be able to do in that sort of position." Josh breathed a sigh of relief then and certainly appreciated her kind words.

"You know, I'm sure I could do the job right," Josh said as he stared out towards the landscape. "But I can never imagine myself leaving Spruce Valley behind. I've come to love this place ever since I came here, and this community really means something to me." Emily admired his words, wondering if she'd ever feel that way about Spruce Valley. She'd come to make some great friends and really appreciate all their kindness to her, but she'd never really felt love towards anything or anyone.

"What do you want for your future then?" Emily asked as she turned her head and looked at him. Their eyes met and Josh thought he'd like to keep her in his future. But for now, he'd keep those thoughts to himself.

"I want to do everything in my power to see Spruce Valley continue to grow," Josh said. "One day, I want to build my own home in town and move out of the apartment above the Sheriff's Office. I want to hire two deputies and really start making sure this town stays safe as it continues to grow."

Emily thought his dream was very admirable and was certain that Josh would be able to accomplish those goals.

"But what about you, Emily? Now that you're here, what do you want for your own future?" Josh asked, pulling Emily from her thoughts.

"That's hard for me to think about anymore," Emily said honestly. "All my life, I was groomed to be a wife and mother. I was tutored so that I'd have the knowledge and skills to land me a wealthy husband." Josh chuckled about this idea and now Emily felt like she could finally laugh about her first thoughts about marriage. "I only ever thought that I'd get married and just listen to whatever my husband said, much like I listened to my father or tutors."

"But you really don't have to listen to anyone but yourself," Josh commented. "So, what do you want to do with yourself?" As Emily looked at Josh, she wondered if he'd be a part of her future. But if she was going to remain as an independent woman, she'd have to really think and act on her own.

"I think it's going to take me some time to discover that for myself," Emily said after a while. "I'm still learning so much that I haven't really thought what I might be good at in order to get some sort of employment to support myself." Josh smiled at her, at least pleased that she was willing to give the idea of working a try.

"I'm sure after a while you'll find something that you'll end up loving in the end," Josh said, hoping to encourage her. "When I was young, I worked on my father's ranch and did the work, but it wasn't what I loved to do. Helping people and stopping bad people from hurting good people is what really got me all stirred up. And I know one day you'll discover that, too." Emily smiled kindly at Josh, glad that he saw so much potential in her. She only hoped that in time she'd come to see the same in herself.

LATER THAT DAY, after Josh had taken her back to the ranch house and enjoyed a cup of coffee with Lucy and Emily at the table as they talked about town gossip, the women were surprised when another visitor came to the house. Emily answered the door when someone knocked, and she opened the door to reveal an older woman with a stern posture but very friendly eyes.

"Good afternoon, my dear. Is Mrs. Slater in?" the woman asked.

"She is," Emily replied. "Might I let her know whom has come to call upon her?"

The older woman smiled as she said, "My name is Mayor Stavros." Emily's eyes went wide as she took in the appearance of the woman. She'd always imagined that mayors were wealthy and wore fancy clothing. But this woman looked like any other member of Spruce Valley.

"Please, come in Madam Mayor," Emily said as she held open the door. She chuckled as she came into the house and hung her cloak on the hook by the door.

"Oh my dear, please address me as Delphina. My husband was the real Mayor of Spruce Valley, and I'm not sure if anyone has called me madam since I was very young," Delphina chuckled. Emily felt a little embarrassed, but as soon as she showed Delphina into the sitting room, her attention soon turned to Lucy who had been sitting in a wing backed chair, working on another gown.

"Delphina, what a pleasant surprise," Lucy said as she looked up to see who had come by. Lucy's feet were up and resting on a stool and a gown sat on her lap with her sewing kit beside her on the floor.

"It's been a while since we've visited, and with you being home and resting, I thought I'd make the trip out to see you," Delphina explained as she took to the chair across from Lucy.

"That is very kind of ye. Have ye met Miss Emily Middleton yet?" Lucy asked as she glanced at Emily as she stood in the doorway, unsure if she should stay or go.

"No, I don't believe I've had the pleasure yet," Delphina replied with a kind smile.

"Well, ye see, Emily here has come to live in Spruce Valley. She's the Sheriff's mail-order-bride," Lucy explained with a smirk. Though Emily often enjoyed being the center of attention, she also didn't want to place any pressure on Josh. She only hoped that he didn't feel any pressure when other people introduced her as his mail-order-bride.

Delphina was surprised to hear this since she often heard all the news in town. She looked quizzically at Emily then, thinking that she was rather beautiful with her dark hair and sparkling blue eyes. She had perfect posture, making Delphina think that this woman was classically educated.

"Can I get you two something to eat or drink?" Emily asked, wanting to be of good use for something.

"We just made some lemonade this morning," Lucy offered as she turned her attention to the Mayor.

"I'd hate to trouble you, but a glass of lemonade does

sound rather good," Delphina agreed. Without hesitation, Emily left the sitting room and walked over to the kitchen. She poured three glasses of lemonade and put together a small plate of maple cookies that had been baked the day before. Emily then returned to the sitting room and distributed the items before finding herself a seat in the rocking chair. Never had Emily thought she'd serve another person, but the task wasn't off-putting. In fact, it was almost a pleasure because Emily had helped in making the lemonade and cookies. It was as though she could show off the products of her own two hands.

"So, Emily, I'd love to know more about you," Delphina said after taking a long sip of her lemonade. "As Mayor of Spruce Valley, I take it upon myself to know everyone in order to best serve the community. Lucy smiled at Delphina as she returned to her needlework. She had guessed that the Mayor had come by after learning about Emily's arrival into town. Though Delphina was an older woman, she had many skills that made her a great mayor. And one of those skills was keeping tabs on everyone. Where Lucy just liked to gossip, Delphina was always thinking about the welfare of everyone in Spruce Valley.

"Well, I'm originally from Atlanta, Georgia," Emily started with. "My father ruined my family's reputation there, so I decided to become a mail-order-bride to hopefully start over with my life." Delphina nodded, understanding that is why most people came to Spruce Valley. They always came running to the West, carrying their hopes and dreams.

"I like that you are honest, Emily," Delphina commented. "It must be difficult for you to admit such things. Your posture alone tells me that you were highly educated." Emily smiled, knowing that old habits would be hard for her to quit. Even in a rocking chair, she still sat up straight.

"My father was a very wealthy man. He spared no expense in my education in the hopes of making me appear more attractive to possible suitors," Emily explained. "I know many modern languages, as well as mathematics, astronomy, economics, and calligraphy."

"My word, that is really impressive," Delphina exclaimed. "I can think of several men in town who could use a calligraphy lesson. I can hardly ever make out their writing." The women giggled at this, and Lucy couldn't help but think of Eddie Murtaugh. When he had first published his mail-order-bride ad, he also needed to improve on his reading and writing skills in order to exchange letters with Fiona.

"Since most of the farmers and cattle hands drop out of school around the eighth grade, most men and women in town don't have a very good education," Lucy added. "It truly is a shame." Delphina nodded her agreement as an idea started to form in her mind.

"Have you ever considered teaching, Emily?" Delphina asked. Emily was surprised by the question. Since she'd never considered any sort of employment before, she had never dreamed of teaching professionally. But as the idea started to form in her head, she reasoned that she'd always enjoyed instructing others. Back in Atlanta, she fondly taught other young ladies her age about fashion and etiquette, as well as what they could honestly get away with in public. It was Emily's way of teaching young ladies that they could have a sense of independence, too.

"I can honestly say I've never considered it before," Emily replied. "I was raised to marry a wealthy husband and never have to worry about working. But since I've come to Spruce Valley, I understand now that employment is not only necessary, but can be enjoyable as well." This caused Delphina to laugh hardily, thinking she'd never really looked at work that way.

"I would have to agree with you, my dear. If you don't love what you do for work, then you'll just regret each day," Delphina said. "But with all your education, if you have a desire to teach others, then I think you should pursue that interest. With Mrs. Crawford also expecting a little one any day now, she'll need someone to fill in for her at the church for the children's lessons."

Emily smiled as she remembered spending part of her day with Mrs. Crawford and all her students. "I do know Mrs. Crawford," Emily said. "On my first day in town, I found it so interesting to see the students gathering in one place for their daily lessons. Since I was privately tutored, I was very curious and did spend some time with her and the children."

"If we are being honest here, then I shall tell you that Mrs. Crawford did speak to me about you coming and visiting with everyone at the church. She was the one who told me that you'd make a good teacher," Delphina confessed.

Lucy chuckled as she shook her head. "Delphina, me dear, I knew there was a real reason for your visit," Lucy said.

"Well, I don't do anything without pure intent and purpose," Delphina agreed. "And when I see a need in the town, I make sure to find a solution as soon as possible." The Mayor then turned her attention back to Emily as she said,

"So, what do you think, Emily? Would you like to try your hand at teaching?"

Emily didn't respond right away. Though the idea filled her with much excitement, she didn't want to be too hasty in her response. There was a lot about teaching she didn't know, even if she did have a lot of education.

"I feel excited about the idea, I do admit," Emily said. "But I'm afraid I don't know much about teaching."

"That part will come naturally as you get used to doing it," Delphina reassured her. "And Mrs. Crawford will be able to direct you. After you've taught for some time, you'll be able to be certified by the state and make things official." Emily was surprised by how easy the Mayor made this all sound. And if she had the Mayor supporting her, Emily figured that she could at least give it a shot.

"Alright then," Emily said, her southern accent coming through in her excitement. "I would be happy to try teaching."

For the remainder of Delphina's visit, the women talked all about teaching and how Emily would be able to get to and from town to accompany Mrs. Crawford for the daily lessons till Emily could take over permanently. At first, Lucy had suggested that she get a ride into town with Martha and Fiona, but after much thought, Emily decided that she'd like to ride her own horse. This had surprised the women, but soon found out that Emily was more daring and bolder than what she appeared to be on the outside.

"We'll talk to Sam and Gray tonight about which horse would be best suited for ye," Lucy said. "I think it's a grand idea that ye'd be willing to ride a horse and be truly independent."

"And I know Mrs. Crawford and the children will be delighted to see you again," Delphina added.

After they had discussed what Emily's pay would be, which she thought was reasonable, Delphina left the ranch house with the promise to come and visit again soon. It only caused them all to chuckle as the older woman left. Lucy went to go lie down after the Mayor left, leaving Emily alone. She was beside herself with how lovely the day had gone. She'd spent the morning with Josh, thinking they were finally starting to see eye-to-eye, and now she had a teaching position in town. It was hard to take it all in and believe, so to make good use of her time, Emily found a piece of writing paper and started to write out a letter to her dear friend, Cynthia.

CHAPTER 13

$\mathcal{N}$erves ran through Emily the next morning as she rose early to help prepare breakfast and then try her hand at riding a horse into town. She wanted to reach town extra early so she could be at the church before the children started to arrive, but that also meant that she needed to get to town first. Thankfully, Dr. Slater would be accompanying her because he also needed to be at the clinic in town for his patients.

"Are ye excited, Emily?" Lucy asked from the head of the table as Emily came in carrying a plate of pancakes and fried eggs. Gray was in the kitchen fixing breakfast and Emily was doing her best to bring it all to the table so the cattle hands could eat and get out into the pasture. It would be calving season soon and they'd need to be on constant watch in case any of the cows needed help birthing. From what had been explained to her, it was the busiest time of the year.

"I sure am," Emily replied as she sat down at the table and

quickly made her plate. "I want to get into town early and maybe even surprise Josh at some point."

"I think that's a great idea," Lucy agreed. She was holding Francene on her lap and convincing the toddler to eat something before she'd go into town with Martha and Fiona. Thankfully, Francene and Samuel got along and normally kept each other occupied. Lucy was really looking forward to giving birth just so she could join everyone in town again.

As soon as Emily was finished eating, she cleaned up her dishes and headed out to the barn after bidding Lucy farewell. She carried a side bag filled with writing paper she promised to pay Dr. Slater back with her first paycheck. She wasn't sure what she'd need, but figured she'd bring at least something. If nothing else, she could use the paper to take notes.

In the barn, Sam showed her how to saddle up one of his older horses that could use the exercise. "Now, he's not going to go real fast, but he's very reliable," Dr. Slater explained.

"I guess I won't be doing any horse racing with him, then," Emily teased as she pulled herself up into the saddle. Sam was impressed that she was able to do so all on her own. He diverted his eyes from her exposed ankles and calves as he mounted his own horse.

"No, there won't be any horse racing for Duncan anymore," Sam replied. "When we were both a bit younger, he was the horse I'd ride when an emergency would come up and I was needed in the dead of night. I won't say he's retired, but he'll make a good riding horse."

"Well, I have faith in Duncan that he won't lead me astray," Emily quipped. Sam laughed as he led them out of the barn. The cattle hands had already saddled up and had ridden out to the pasture, so the morning seemed almost quiet as they rode out of the barn. The sounds of cattle in the distance rose into the air, and though the smell of the ranch had first made Emily a little leery of being out on the ranch, she'd gotten used to the smell and almost considered it homey.

Together, Sam and Emily rode into town at a gallop. Though she wasn't about to push Duncan, she was at least pleased that the older horse could keep up with the mare that Sam was riding. She thoroughly enjoyed the feeling of riding and was sure she'd look forward to the end of the school day just so she could ride home. The morning sun was still peeking over the horizon, sending shades of blue and pink through the sky. With this being the first day of her teaching, or at least learning to, she couldn't have imagined a more perfect morning.

They slowed their horses to a trot as they entered town. Sam bid her good luck before making his way to the clinic. After thanking him, she led Duncan down the main street till she reached the church just outside of town on the north end. She had passed by the Sheriff's Office on her way and for a moment she thought about stopping and saying hello to Josh. But on her very first day, Emily did not want to be late.

When she reached the church, Emily took her time dismounting from the horse. She was grateful that Duncan was such a strong horse for his age and seemed to handle her awkward movements as she set foot on the ground once more. She then took his reins and tethered him on the hitching post before walking up the stairs to the church.

Seeing that the front door was opened, Emily stepped right inside. Though she didn't see Mrs. Crawford, she did see a couple sitting in the front pew with their heads bowed. Emily felt like she'd just stepped into a room she shouldn't have and was just about to turn around and leave when Mrs. Crawford came walking slowly up the steps.

"Ah, good morning, Emily," Mrs. Crawford said once she reached the top of the steps. She took a deep breath and let it out slowly. "This baby is going to be the death of me!" she chuckled.

"Good morning, Reverend. Mrs. Gibbons," Mrs. Crawford said as she continued into the church. The couple looked up when they saw Mrs. Crawford coming in.

"Ah, good morning, Mrs. Crawford," said the man as he stood. Emily followed close behind Mrs. Crawford, not wanting to appear rude. She figured it would be wise for her to meet the reverend and his wife since she'd be teaching in their church.

"May I introduce you to the new schoolteacher, Miss Emily Middleton," Mrs. Crawford said as she gestured to Emily. "She's been classically trained in Georgia and will make an excellent addition to the classroom."

"Ah, Miss Middleton. It's a pleasure to meet you," Mrs. Gibbons said. She was an older woman with blonde hair and a round figure. But her smile was her defining feature. She appeared very kind and welcoming. "You'll soon meet our three children. Henry, Timothy, and Jessica."

"I'm looking forward to visiting with all of the children once more," Emily said. "I had come by one day before and was eager to see so many coming together for their daily lessons. I was privately tutored and find this setting much more enjoyable."

"Well, we are just pleased to hear that Mrs. Crawford will have someone with her during the day," the reverend spoke up. "No offense, Mrs. Crawford, but it seems that you'll pop any day."

"No offense taken, Reverend," Mrs. Crawford said with a chuckle. She sat down heavily onto a chair near a desk that had been placed at the front of the church to be used for teaching. On Sunday's, the desk and chair were removed and replaced by the pulpit for the reverend to deliver his weekly sermons.

"We'll get out of your hair now and send the children over shortly," Mrs. Gibbons said as the two of them left the church. "Have a good day."

"They are such a lovely couple," Mrs. Crawford commented once they were gone. "It's so kind of them to let us use the church for these lessons."

Before the children arrived that morning, Mrs. Crawford did her best to get Emily caught up on what all the children were currently learning and working on. It was a lot for Emily to take in because even though she understood what Mrs. Crawford was teaching the children, it was hard to keep track of every student and their current progress.

"With your helping out, we'll be able to focus on the children's needs individually. There are a few I'm worried about reaching high enough marks to go on to the next grade," Mrs. Crawford explained. "And with this little one coming any day, I want to make sure the students are ready for this transition."

"Don't worry, Mrs. Crawford. Even though I am not certified by the state, I am eager to help these children succeed and to teach them all I know," Emily said with much conviction in her voice. Mrs. Crawford smiled, feeling reassured.

"And that's what makes a teacher great. Her passion and concern for her students," Mrs. Crawford declared. With Emily just starting out, she wanted to prove to everyone that she could not only teach but do a good job at it as well. She needed to prove to herself that she could really enjoy working, and perhaps even show Josh that she could be his ideal wife.

Emily had little time to think as the children started to arrive at the church. She followed Mrs. Crawford's instructions as she rang the church bell, signaling that school was starting for the day. Emily loved seeing all the happy children as they came running into the building and were quick to find their spots in the pews as they all sat together with those of similar ages. Emily was also surprised when she saw several Indian children from the local Crow Tribe also attending. It wasn't long before Emily was caught up on the daily lessons, helping each child to improve and understand the lessons for the day.

SAM CAME into the Sheriff's Office carrying a picnic basket of food that he'd picked up from The Eatery. He set it on Josh's desk where he was busy filling out a few papers in response to an inquiry from a nearby sheriff. Josh was always willing to help local authorities track down criminals and Josh was trying to remember all the characteristics of a burglar he'd helped bring to jail a few years back, who may be back at it again. But when Sam set the picnic basket on his desk, he was forced to look up at the doctor and try to figure out what the meaning of all of this was.

"I'm flattered, Sam, I really am. But I don't really have time to go on a picnic with you right now," Josh said with a smirk. He really did not want to lose his train of thought right now, but figured he could pay his best friend some attention for a moment.

"Josh, this isn't for me. It's for Emily," Sam said with a chuckle. "I thought you two might enjoy lunch together."

"Sam, I think that's a great idea, but I don't have time to ride out to the ranch right now with this report I need to fill out for another sheriff. We might have a repeat crime in Montana and I want to make sure I telegram this back to him today," Josh explained, starting to feel frustrated. He appreciated what Sam was trying to do for him, but he simply didn't have the time today.

"Well, then it's a good thing that Emily is now working with Mrs. Crawford on schooling the children and not all the way at the ranch," Sam said with a wicked grin, finding himself very amusing. His plan worked as Josh stilled and looked at him as though he didn't believe him.

"Emily took a job as a schoolteacher?" Josh asked, wondering if he'd heard Sam wrong.

"She sure did. I guess she made a real good impression on Mrs. Crawford and the Mayor. Seems she has the education if not the skill. But Mrs. Crawford says she has real potential," Sam explained, pleased as punch for coming up with this idea.

"Well I'll be damned," Josh said as he looked down at his report. "Sam, let me get this done real fast and I'll be sure to head over to the church to see for myself."

"Sounds like a mighty fine plan, if I do say so myself," Sam said with a chuckle as he moved towards the door.

"Yes, thank you, Sam," Josh said in a sarcastic voice as the doctor left the Sheriff's Office. Josh did his best to focus on the task at hand as he finished the report and then took it and the basket over to Frost's to send over the telegram. Once that was finished, he speedily went over to the church to see for himself what Emily was up to.

As he came over to the church with the basket in hand, he saw Emily and Mrs. Crawford standing outside the church while the children played during their break. He saw the way she smiled as she watched the kids closely. She laughed when they convinced her to play tag with them, and as he watched her picking up the hem of her gown and chase after them, he thought he'd never seen anything so beautiful before. The fact that she was willing to play with children really warmed his heart.

"Good day, Sheriff," Mrs. Crawford said as he came up to the church. He took his eyes off Emily only for a moment to say hello to the schoolteacher.

"I heard that there was a new teacher in town," Josh said as he watched Emily play with the children.

"Oh yes, there sure is," Mrs. Crawford confirmed. "And she's really good with the children, as you can see."

"Had to see it to believe it," Josh stated. A few minutes later, Emily looked up to see Josh standing there, a funny smile on his face. She stopped immediately and rubbed her hands down her gown to smooth and straighten it out. She almost felt embarrassed for what she had been doing, but as she smiled down at the children as they all ran to tag her, she figured that she couldn't help it. Though she might be their teacher, she also wanted them to know that she was also a person they could come to when they needed help with something.

After she encouraged the children to go play without her, she approached Josh. She noticed how he was carrying a basket in his hands and wondered what idea he had.

"Hello, Josh," Emily said as she walked up to him. "How is your day going?"

"It's been busy, but a little birdie told me about the new schoolteacher in town," Josh said, his lopsided grin appearing. It made Emily weak in the knees and she did her best to keep her composure in front of the children. "I figured I'd come see for myself and ask if you'd care to join me for some lunch." Emily didn't reply but looked to Mrs. Crawford, who nodded in response.

"The children and I will be fine on our own for a bit," Mrs. Crawford said before she turned and made her way up the stairs. There, she rung the church bell, signaling for the children to come back inside for the afternoon lesson.

"Well, let's have a seat over here," Emily said as she pointed to the base of a tree. It looked shaded and comfortable enough to sit and enjoy some food.

"Ladies first," Josh gestured. Emily smiled as she led the way over to the tree. As they settled down, Josh started to pull out the food that Sam had gotten for them. He couldn't help but smirk at it all, thinking that Sam had really outdone himself this time.

"So, you said you've had a busy morning?" Emily

inquired, hoping to start some sort of conversation between them while they ate.

"Yes, I had to fill out a report this morning," Josh said as he dished out plates of food for them both. It all looked delicious as he portioned out fresh rolls, baked chicken, and buttery green beans. "A nearby sheriff reached out to other officers in Montana. He's on the lookout for a bank robber matching a few descriptions I remember from a burglar I nabbed a few years back. I would have been by earlier if I hadn't needed to finish that report as soon as possible."

"I completely understand, Josh," Emily reassured. "It's simply nice to get to spend some time with you." Josh nodded, appreciating Emily's understanding of the demands of his position in town.

"But enough about me. Tell me more about you," Josh said with a smile. "I was surprised when I heard that you'd taken the teaching job." Emily sighed as she nodded, remembering some of their previous conversations.

"I really took into consideration what you said about finding something that you're passionate about. I really didn't think that employment could ever be something that someone enjoyed," Emily admitted. "When I met with Delphina, she encouraged me to consider the position because of my extensive education. And since I've always enjoyed instructing others, I figured that I could give it a shot." Emily was a little nervous about what Josh would say in response and for a moment, simply concentrated on the food. It was delicious, and since she'd eaten so quickly that morning, she was rather famished.

Josh thought that Emily had come a long way since

arriving in Spruce Valley. He could see that she was starting to bloom in the community and that she was starting to put her mind towards becoming the person she probably always wanted to be. It only took some encouragement to see that she had all this hidden potential, if only she was willing to give different things a try.

"I think you'll come to enjoy teaching just as much as I enjoy being a sheriff," Josh said after a while. "I saw the way you were with the children today and the fact that you're willing to play with them means that you actually care about them." Emily was beyond pleased to hear Josh's remarks. She really wanted to impress him, along with the rest of the community.

"I would have given anything to have learned my lessons with other students," Emily admitted. "I want these children to know they are not only going to get the help they need to succeed, but also be able to rely on their teacher. I don't want to be just an instructor. I want to be someone people can come to if they need help with their education." Emily could hardly believe the words that were coming out of her mouth. It was as though as she spoke, the truth of her heart came out. She never knew that she had this desire before until she was willing to give it a try.

"Well, it sounds like you have the passion needed for the position," Josh said. "And I'm sure in time, you'll get used to all the different demands of teaching."

"Yes, I will admit that today has been quite overwhelming as I learn how Mrs. Crawford keeps everyone and everything organized," Emily said with a chuckle. "And after I've gained some new skills, I'll be able to apply to be certified."

"Won't that be something," Josh encouraged. Emily nodded, thinking that she'd enjoy having the title of certified schoolteacher. She never thought a woman could ever be a teacher, but Mrs. Crawford would surely teach her more than how to teach. Emily would also learn how to be a successful, independent woman.

"Well, I should be getting back to the students," Emily said as she helped Josh pack up the picnic basket. "But thank you for coming by and bringing lunch."

"Any time," Josh said as he helped Emily to her feet. "We'll have to do this again soon when we can find time between both our work schedules." Emily thought it was rather interesting to think about having a work schedule. It pleased her no end as she parted with Josh. She was eager to return to the students and continue learning all she could about teaching effectively.

CHAPTER 14

*J*osh realized that after three weeks of watching Emily continue to progress in this new teaching position that he was more attracted to her than he'd ever been before. Though Josh had first been drawn to her beauty, he was now more impressed with her mind. Not only had Emily been attending every school day and assisting Mrs. Crawford, but she'd also been tutoring different adults in the evenings over at The Eatery. And now that Mrs. Crawford had gone into labor and delivered a beautiful baby girl, Emily had taken over as lead teacher and was conducting the daily lessons all on her own.

Though it had been harder to be alone with Emily, he'd made time to see her during the day. Sometimes he'd bring her lunch or dinner, knowing that it was a long ride back to the ranch every evening. Every once in a while they'd have dinner at The Eatery and Josh would escort her back to the ranch and come back in the evening. It might seem like a lot of running around, but Josh was really starting to enjoy spending time with the new Emily.

When she'd first come to Spruce Valley, she'd been very set in her old ways. So much so that she had unrealistic expectations of married life. But as he slowly showed her what it was like to live in the West, Emily had slowly adapted to the lifestyle. She'd not only learned the basics of riding a horse and cooking, but also housework, and now a teaching position in town as well. It had only been about two months since her arrival to Spruce Valley and already she'd accomplished so much in such a short time.

The other thing Josh noticed was the way she attracted the attention of other men. Though everyone knew that Emily had come to Spruce Valley as a mail-order-bride for him, Josh knew that there were a few bold men who wouldn't mind trying their luck with Emily as well. Josh knew that the time had come for him to make his final move with Emily. He thought they had come a long way since first meeting in person and now might be the time to make things official.

That evening, Josh had something special planned for Emily. He'd invited her over for dinner and planned to cook her a good meal. He wanted Emily to see his small apartment above the Sheriff's Office because if they did marry, they'd be living together in this space. He had all sorts of things he wanted to tell Emily and hoped that tonight would be the night he'd finally tell her all his hopes and dreams. Josh felt a little vulnerable with putting himself out there, but his gut told him that everything would work out in the end.

Josh was busy in the kitchen, stirring a pot of creamy potato chowder on the stove when he heard a knock on the door below. Moving the pot over to the part of the stove that didn't have a small fire burning below, Josh hurried down the stairs into the Sheriff's Office and quickly pulled open the door. Before him stood Emily. She'd dressed in a very fashionable gown, the purple silk shimmering in the setting sun. She'd curled her long black hair and pinned it to the top of her head, exposing her long and slender neck. She was every bit the Atlanta debutante she'd been born as, but as Josh looked into her blue eyes, he could see the real Emily before him.

"Come on in," Josh said with a smile, opening the door all the way and allowing Emily to enter.

"Thank you," Emily replied as she stepped into the office. It was the first time Emily had been in the office and she found it very plain and simple. The only thing that was in the office was Josh's desk and chair. Another desk and chair had been pushed up against the opposite wall and appeared to be waiting for a deputy one day. But there were no comforting touches, even though Emily figured that a Sheriff's Office wasn't meant to be warm and welcoming.

"Right this way," Josh said, pulling Emily's attention back to him. "The apartment is right up these stairs." Emily followed his lead and took the stairs slowly. There wasn't much light, but as soon as they came through the door at the top of the stairs, she found the apartment to be a lot more welcoming than the office downstairs. What further surprised Emily was that there was an older couple sitting at the small dining table in the middle of the space. When Josh had invited her over for dinner at his apartment, she hadn't been expecting anyone else.

"Emily, may I introduce you to my parents. This is my

mother, Matilda Ryder. And my father, Joshua Ryder," Josh introduced as the older couple stood. Emily was taken back by being introduced to his parents. She certainly hadn't been expecting this and called on her years of concealing her inner emotions as she shook hands with them both.

"It's a pleasure to meet you both," Emily said as she greeted them. She watched the way they observed her, and for a moment Emily wished she'd dressed in something a little plainer. She had really wanted to look her best for tonight since this would be the first time coming to Josh's home. But now she would have liked to have known what Josh had planned for them before arriving this evening.

"It's nice to meet you as well," Matilda spoke up when her husband continued to scrutinize the woman with his eyes. "Josh has told us so many things about you already." They all settled down at the table as Josh returned to the stove. Emily had an instinct to help him with the meal but wondered if it would be better to remain at the table and entertain his parents.

"I am pleased to hear this," Emily replied, making sure to keep a steady smile on her face. "Josh has explained to me that you two live a little south of Spruce Valley on the family ranch."

"Yes. Our family has been ranching for four generations. That is, until Junior decided to play law," Joshua said, glancing at his son for a moment before returning his gaze to Emily. She was a beauty, that he could admit. But he didn't trust people from wealthy families.

"One of the first things I learned about Josh is how passionate he is about being the Sheriff of Spruce Valley," Emily said proudly. She had detected the hints of tension in

Mr. Ryder's voice and wanted to show how highly she thought of Josh. "After coming to stay here, I learned how this community really thinks highly of Josh and all the good work he's done here." Matilda smiled at Emily, finding it nice to hear so many good things about her son.

"When we got a copy of the article where Josh was detailed a hero, I couldn't be prouder," Matilda said as she looked to her son. He looked over his shoulder at her, grateful to hear such a compliment from his mother.

"He really become quite famous, even in the East where I'm from," Emily agreed. "When I saw his ad in the paper, I almost couldn't believe that a man like Josh would need help in finding a wife." They chuckled over this, but Emily saw that Mr. Ryder hardly cracked a smile.

"I bet you were eager to send Josh a letter then," Joshua spoke up, seeing if he could catch Emily in any ill will towards his son.

"I will admit that I was intrigued why a famous sheriff would be writing a mail-order-bride ad. It is only one of the things that piqued my interest about Josh. But I wouldn't say it was the leading reason," Emily said very clearly, hoping to prove her point that she wasn't after Josh just because he was famous. Though her ideas about Josh were muddled and unrealistic in the beginning, she now saw Josh for who he truly was.

"Ma, I've made your favorite," Josh said as he came to the table with several bowls.

"Ah, how thoughtful of you, Josh," Matilda said, delighted to see the potato soup.

"Whenever I got sick, Ma would always make potato soup

for me. It wasn't until I was older that I learned it was her favorite," Josh said to Emily, thinking that it was nice to have his parents visiting this week, and also have them meet his intended.

"My goodness, did he eat as a child," Matilda said with a chuckle. "I remember the one time he ate a whole pot of potato soup all on his own." Josh brought over the loaf of bread he'd made earlier in the day, proud of being able to make dinner for everyone.

"If it doesn't have a good amount of cheese, it doesn't taste right," Joshua said as he started to eat with gusto. Josh was put off by this, having wanted to say grace before they began. Seeming to notice Josh's discomfort, Emily bowed her head and said a silent prayer before beginning to eat.

"I've had jambalaya before, but nothing quite as creamy as this," Emily said. "I understand why you'd eat a whole pot of it."

"Well, I'm sure my mother has lots of interesting details about my childhood that she'd be happy to share with you," Josh said with a chuckle.

"Miss Middleton, where are your parents?" Joshua asked between bites. Josh scowled at his father then. "What did I say?" he asked in mocked hurt.

"Mr. Ryder, my mother died giving birth to me," Emily said as she stiffened. "And my father disappeared after he ruined our family name when he destroyed his own business." The room fell silent as Emily poked at her food, feeling a bit embarrassed having to share these particular details with Josh's parents upon first meeting them.

"Well, I think it's lovely that you'd travel all the way out here on your own and make a name for yourself," Matilda spoke up after a while.

"Emily has started working as a schoolteacher here in town," Josh added. "Mrs. Crawford just had her baby, so Emily came into town right at the perfect time to make sure the children continue on with their lessons."

"Wouldn't have expected a woman such as yourself to be eager to find a working job," Joshua then commented, making Emily's heart drop even further. She wasn't sure why Josh's father was being so hard on her, but she wasn't about to crumble under the pressure.

"You're absolutely right, Mr. Ryder. I had no designs to ever work a day in my life," Emily said in a sing-song voice. "But your son taught me not only the importance of having a job, but also that it could bring passion and purpose to one's life as well. I've come to enjoy teaching more than I ever thought I would, and I'm glad that Josh has been such a big example in my life of what it means to work for a living." Matilda smiled at Emily, thinking she was witty and quick on her feet. She wasn't sure why her husband was being so cross with Emily, but she planned to give him a piece of her mind later.

Joshua harrumphed as he finished eating, scraping the sides of his bowl with his bread. Josh was glaring at his father, trying to wrap his mind around why the man was giving Emily such a hard time. He was starting to think that this dinner had been a bad idea, and if his father kept this up, he was going to send his parents' home early.

After they'd finished eating and the table had been cleared, Matilda and Emily took care of the dishes as they talked quietly with one another. Emily talked about how much she was enjoying being a schoolteacher and Matilda shared details about Josh when he was little. They laughed quietly together, and from where Josh was sitting in the living room, he couldn't help but smile to see them so happy. He looked at his father then, wanting to figure out why the man had picked a bone tonight.

"What gives, Pa?" Josh asked in a soft voice, not wanting to draw attention to him.

"I don't know what you're talking about," Joshua said as he puffed on his pipe, eager to get out of the small apartment and back to the inn. He couldn't understand why his son continued to live in such a small space instead of building a house or moving home.

"You do know what I'm talking about, Pa. You're giving Emily the ninth degree," Josh said, becoming more frustrated that his father wouldn't even admit to what he'd done during dinner.

"I just think that you could do better, Josh, that's all," Joshua finally said. "It's not like she's some nice country girl who can actually deal with being a sheriff's wife."

"And what makes you think I can't handle it?" Emily asked, coming to join them in the living room. They'd finished cleaning up the kitchen right as Mr. Ryder had spoken, and Emily couldn't stand his negative attitude any longer. Joshua didn't like how Emily was challenging him and figured he'd put her in her place once and for all.

"Because a young lady such as yourself is more fit for tea parties and balls," Joshua said as he got to his feet. "The first time Josh gets called away on a dangerous job, you're going to be so filled with fear and worry that you won't be able to handle it again." Emily didn't like the way the man had raised his voice or the dagger eyes he was giving her. And since she didn't need to tolerate any of this, she picked up the hem of her gown and promptly made her way out of the apartment and down the stairs.

"Emily, wait!" Josh called after her, but Emily only quickened her pace. And as she did so, she stumbled over her feet because it was so dark on the staircase and went tumbling down the stairs. By the time she hit the floor in the office, she'd completely passed out from being knocked unconscious.

"Oh, God. No! Emily, no!" Josh hollered, terrified that she'd fallen and twisted her neck. But as he came running down the stairs, he reached her body and felt her chest to confirm that she was still breathing.

"Josh, is she okay?" Matilda asked as she came down the stairs slowly with a lantern in her hand.

"She's hurt bad, Ma," Josh said as he looked up the stairs at his mother. Matilda could see tears in his eyes as she looked down at her terrified son.

"It's going to be okay, Josh," Matilda said as she finished coming down the stairs. She looked down at Emily and saw how pale she'd turned. "I'm going to stay here with her and you're going to go get the doc."

"But what happens when I leave and she passes away?" Josh asked. "Mama, I can't lose her. I love her."

"Josh, you listen to me real well," Matilda said. "You go get that doc and you get your butt back here. I'm not going to let Emily die." Matilda gave her son a stern look, hoping he'd jump into action. Josh looked down at Emily one last time before pushing himself to his feet and running out of the Sheriff's Office. He didn't even bother closing the door as he ran into the night, moving as fast as he could over to the livery stables so he could collect his mare and get to the Slater's ranch as fast as possible. He prayed under his breath over and over again, pleading with the Lord to not let Emily pass away.

CHAPTER 15

At first, Emily didn't understand what was happening. Her mind had still held onto the anger that had coursed through her body after what Mr. Ryder had said to her. But now that anger seemed to be transformed into some sort of fire that was raging through her body.

"We've got to get her body cooled down," she heard a familiar voice say. "The fever is making her too hot and the swelling in her head needs to come down."

"What do you need me to do?" came another voice.

"Let's strip her and start bathing her in cold water," said the first voice.

"Seems like a woman's job," came a third voice.

"Yeah, let us do it."

Emily could tell that she was surrounded by people but couldn't make out any of their faces. She tried her best to open her eyes, but the effort felt like too much for her to handle. Instead, she drifted back off to sleep, thinking it would be better to fall back into unconsciousness instead of feeling all this pain.

When she came to again, she felt different. The fire seemed to be gone, but now the pain was stronger. Her headed pounded with pain, but as she tried to raise her hand to cradle her head, she found that she couldn't do so. Just trying to move her right arm only caused more pain to erupt in that area. Emily desperately wished she knew what was happening to her, but as the pain increased, it only brought her deeper down into slumber.

Emily wasn't sure for how long or how many days this pattern had been going on. But eventually, she found the strength to open her eyes. As her eyes adjusted to the dim lit room, she saw that she was in a small room she'd never been in before. She was resting on a bed, that much she could tell. Her left hand moved, her fingers brushing against soft fabrics. She looked down her body to see that she'd been changed into a nightgown and she didn't like the idea of someone having changed her clothes.

But modesty seemed to be the last of her concerns. As she tried to move her right arm, she found it very difficult to do so. She turned her head to look down that side of her body and saw that her forearm had been placed in a cast and was too heavy for her to do very much with. She sighed, trying to remember what had happened to have landed her in this state.

When Emily tried to sit up, a pounding erupted in her head. Her vision blurred and for a moment she thought she was going to pass out again. But she closed her eyes to the pain and willed it to go away. Sitting up, she took several deep breaths. Then, she realized she wasn't alone.

Sitting in a wooden chair in the corner she saw Josh with slouched shoulders and his head resting back against the wall. His face looked as though he hadn't shaved in days, but he appeared so peaceful as he was sleeping. Emily hated the thought of waking him, but she was dying of thirst and seriously needed to use a water closet.

"Josh," Emily whispered, her voice sounding rough from not having anything to drink in however long it had been since she'd been injured. But she was loud enough to cause Josh to stir. It took him a moment to realize that Emily was not only awake but sitting up on her own.

"Dear Lord, Emily. Don't sit up," Josh said as he sprung from the chair and came to sit next to her. "You shouldn't sit up until Dr. Slater comes to check on you."

"Josh, water," Emily said, refusing to lie down anymore. Josh was quick to pour her a small cup of water from a pitcher on a nearby table and handed it to Emily, fearful about her sitting up already. Emily took the cup carefully and drank till it was empty, the water refreshing her throat immediately.

"Now please, Emily, you really should be resting," Josh insisted as he took the cup from her and set it aside.

"I need to use the water closet and I need to know what happened. Where am I?" Emily asked, continuing to be persistent. Josh couldn't believe how stubborn she was being but couldn't really fault her after everything that had happened.

"Emily, you're in the clinic in town," Josh started with. "And you've been here for almost three days now." Emily stilled at hearing she'd been asleep for three days. Her mind raced, trying to remember all that had happened to lead her to being placed in the clinic. She moved her right arm slowly, just raising it a bit to figure out why it had been casted and how broken it could be.

"I don't remember anything," Emily stated. "I don't remember getting into an accident." Emily's words pierced Josh's heart. He felt guilty enough and hated to be the one to tell her the truth. But it was only fair that he was the one to tell her.

"You were having dinner over at my apartment with my parents. I had invited you over and surprised you with meeting my parents," Josh explained slowly. "But my father was being bull-headed and said some things he shouldn't have. You left in a hurry but stumbled and fell down the stairs."

"I guess I must have tried to break my fall," Emily said as she looked down at her right hand. "But it doesn't sound real, to be honest."

"My parents are still in town," Josh said. "And my father would like to apologize." Emily only nodded, uneasy about the idea of being seen in this condition. But as she remembered that she'd been undressed and changed into a night-gown, it seemed that she had no reason to really feel embarrassed anymore.

"Does the clinic have a water closet?" Emily asked, really feeling like she needed to heed the call of nature.

"Yes. I'll help you use it," Josh said as he stood and then slowly helped Emily to her feet. As she put weight on her feet, Emily's head spun with dizziness. She closed her eyes a moment as she gripped onto Josh with her good hand. When it passed, she opened her eyes, ungripped her hand and walked slowly. Josh helped her out of the room and down the hallway.

After she'd finished her business on her own, she allowed

Josh to take some of her weight as she slowly made her way back to the bed. She couldn't believe how weak her body felt, but was at least glad she was able to get cleaned up a bit. As Josh lowered her back onto the bed, Emily sat up and took a few deep breaths before allowing Josh to guide her down to a resting position on the bed.

"I feel like I just ran for miles," Emily said as she closed her eyes briefly.

"Dr. Slater said that it will take some time to heal. But the fact that you're awake is a good sign," Josh said, looking down at her with concern.

"Did he think I wouldn't wake?" Emily asked, fearing the answer.

"You hit your head pretty hard," Josh said as he winced at her question. "Sam said your brain was swelling bad and there was a chance you'd never wake up from the coma." Emily sighed heavily, thinking that the fall down the stairs had to be a lot worse than what she'd first imagined.

"Well, I'm awake for now," Emily said. "I just feel so exhausted." Josh nodded, even though she still had her eyes closed.

"Are you hungry?" Josh asked, wondering what more he could do for her.

"I'm not, but I'm sure after three days I should eat something," Emily said. A knock on the door was heard and Josh rose from the side of the bed and quickly answered it. He was surprised when he opened the door and saw Bright Star standing on the other side.

"I've brought some things for Emily Middleton that might be of use," Bright Star explained when he saw the confusion in the Sheriff's eyes. He held up a bag to show him what he'd brought, and Josh thought it all smelled funny. But not wanting to offend the Indian, Josh opened the door and bid him enter.

"Emily, Bright Star has come to visit with you," Josh said as he returned to the edge of her bed. Bright Star kneeled beside the bed and looked at Emily with great concern. Emily opened her eyes briefly and tried to give the Indian a kind smile.

"I don't think I'll be able to play poker today," Emily quipped. Bright Star chuckled as he started to pull various things out of his deerskin bag.

"No, not today, Emily Middleton. But very soon, I assure you," Bright Star said as he pulled a salve from his bag and handed it to Josh. "This should be rubbed into the skin to help it heal faster."

"Thank you," Josh said, wondering if Emily would allow him to apply it later. He'd feel more comfortable asking Martha or Fiona to apply it when they next came to visit the clinic. Everyone had been into the clinic every day to check on Emily's progress and they would all be relieved to learn that she'd at least woken up.

"Now, here is some medicine that is meant to be put onto the gums of the mouth. It will help with the pain and a sour stomach," Bright Star explained. He scooped what looked like mud onto his fingers and promptly opened Emily's mouth just wide enough to where he could rub it onto her gums. She furrowed her brows but didn't protest, finding the substance to at least be flavorful, if not strange feeling.

"And next, I shall sing a special prayer for you," Bright

Star announced as he rubbed fresh herbs together in his hands and moved them above Emily's body as he started to say a chant that Josh didn't understand. The air was filled with the smell of mint and rosemary, which Josh thought was at least pleasant smelling. He remained silent during Bright Star's chant, trying to keep a positive attitude about what the Indian was doing when he was a Christian man. Josh figured that it was the thought that counted.

"Emily Middleton will be sure to heal faster now," Bright Star said as he finished his prayer and began to gather his things again. "This pouch contains more of the medicine for her mouth. Give it to her when she's in pain."

"Thank you, Bright Star," Josh said as the Indian got to his feet. Bright Star grunted his approval before leaving the room. It was almost like he'd never been there, but as Josh looked down at the items in his hands, he felt grateful for them.

"How are you feeling, Emily?" Josh asked, but Emily had already fallen back to sleep. Bright Star's chanting had encouraged her back to sleep and the pain in her body had seemed to fade away for a moment. Josh smiled as he brushed back a strand of her long black hair from her face, at least happy to see that she was resting well again.

Setting the items on the side table, Josh returned to his chair and decided that it would be a good idea for him to catch a few more hours of sleep himself. His constant worrying had kept him up all night and now he was completely exhausted. He only hoped that Emily waking for a short time was a good sign that she would one day make a full recovery.

~

I<small>T</small> <small>WAS</small> five days after Emily had first regained consciousness till she was fit to leave the clinic. She was still weak and slow to move, but knew that she wasn't going to feel her old self again until she got back to the things she enjoyed doing. Wanting to be closer to the church to resume lessons with the children, Emily had her things moved back to the Honeywell Inn. That way she wouldn't have to worry about riding till her arm fully healed. And though the Slaters were sad to hear the news, they completely understood.

In the mornings, it took Emily a lot of time to get ready for the day. Dressing herself with only one arm was frustrating, and every time she bumped her bad arm, it would send shocks of pain along the full length of it. By the time she was done dressing, she felt exhausted and would often need to sit for a moment before she could get up and move about again. Eventually, she returned to the church to oversee the children's lessons. Thankfully, Reverend Paul and his wife had at least been at the church when the children arrived for the day and allowed the students to review basic lessons. Emily was grateful to the couple and hoped that she would be able to make it up to them one day.

The hardest part of recovering from the fall was the memories that slowly came back to her. Eventually she regained everything and remembered the words that Mr. Ryder had said to her. After everything she'd been able to accomplish since coming to Spruce Valley, she wasn't sure how she was going to show her worth to Josh's father and therefore she started to doubt her own abilities. Even though Emily was back on her feet, she hadn't gone out of her way to spend any time with Josh in fear of running into his parents again. This had proved particularly difficult since his parents were staying at the same inn as she was. So far, they hadn't run into each other—yet. And though Emily very much liked Josh's mother, she didn't want to have to look Mr. Ryder in the eyes again.

Emily thought all had been going well for a few weeks. She went back to teaching when one day she went into The Eatery for dinner and found Josh and his parents were also patrons for the evening. She did her best to avoid them and found a table at the back of the room. She then picked up her menu and pretended to be interested in it to avoid any awkward eye contact. But when someone took the seat next to her, she knew that she wasn't going to be able to avoid them forever.

"Why, hello there, Miss. I don't think we've met before," came Josh's voice. She couldn't help but smirk as she set down her menu and looked at him. "Because I know if we had met before, you wouldn't have come and sat all alone back here."

"I just didn't want to interrupt anything," Emily said, her eyes locking with Josh's. She'd missed seeing his honey colored eyes and the lopsided grin on his face. She sighed, feeling more comfortable then she had in a while.

"You wouldn't have been interrupting at all," Josh said as he carefully took her right hand in his. "It's always worth getting to spend any amount of time with you, and I know you're still recovering and getting back into the swing of teaching again."

"Well, I appreciate your consideration," Emily said.. "Dr. Slater said that by winter my arm should be fully healed."

Another wave of guilt washed over Josh and now he could no longer bear it.

"Emily, I want you to come have dinner with me and my folks. My father has something he'd like to say to you," Josh said. Emily stiffened, thinking that Mr. Ryder had already said quite enough to her.

"I don't know if I can handle anything more your father has to say to me," Emily admitted as she looked away from Josh. But when he gently squeezed her fingers, she forced herself to look Josh in the eyes once more.

"You're one of the strongest women I know, Emily. You should never back down from a challenge," Josh said with a smirk on his lips. Emily couldn't help but smile herself, thinking that what he said was very true. But ever since the accident, she'd been a lot more mindful of herself and hadn't really tried anything but what she needed to do to survive.

"Alright then," Emily eventually agreed. She allowed Josh to pull back her chair so she could stand with ease. And then Josh led her over to his table as both his parents rose to their feet. Joshua pulled off his hat as Emily came near, the knots in his stomach gathered together as he started to wring his hat between his hands.

"Miss Middleton, I'd just like to say that I'm very sorry for everything that happened. I should have never been quick to judge you like that," Joshua said, his eyes filled with guilt. It was clear to Emily that he felt sorry about the situation and she hoped the man wouldn't give her anymore trouble in the future.

"I appreciate your apology," Emily replied calmly.

"Would you care to join us for dinner then?" Joshua asked hopefully.

"Yes, I would like that," she responded. Joshua gave her a quick smile as they all settled down at the table. They ordered the special of the day and Emily enjoyed some of Nell's splendid tea.

"It's good to see you out and about again, Miss Middleton," Nell said as she poured Emily's tea.

"Thank you, Nell," Emily replied. The woman gave her a wink before moving to another table. It was hard to believe all that had happened since coming to Spruce Valley. But even with a broken arm, she was pleased with where her life was headed. During the dinner, Emily snuck peeks at Josh, thinking he was as handsome as ever. She only hoped that she could continue to prove her worth to him.

After they'd finished dinner, Josh invited her to walk with him. Emily agreed and they said goodbye to his parents as they returned to the inn. With her left arm hanging on Josh's, he led her through town and a bit away from it as they watched the sun dip below the horizon, filling the sky with waves of orange. The weather was growing warmer with signs that soon spring would give way to summer.

"I heard today that Dr. Slater was called home for an emergency," Josh said at one point, causing fear to spread over Emily.

"My goodness, what has happened? Why didn't you tell me before?" Emily asked quickly.

"Don't worry, Emily," Josh said with a chuckle. "Lucy gave birth to another girl is all." Emily sighed deeply, thinking she should have thought about that first before jumping to conclusions. "I would have told you sooner if something bad had happened."

"I'm so sorry, Josh. I should have known as much," Emily said. "So, Sam and Lucy now are parents of two girls?" This made Josh chuckle as he shook his head.

"Seems like the men of Slater Ranch are soon going to be outnumbered," Josh reasoned. "But it really has me thinking about something."

"Oh? And what's that?" Emily wondered as she watched the sunset, thinking it was nice to simply stand with a handsome man and enjoy something so wonderful and beautiful.

"That someday soon I'd like a little one of my own," Josh declared as he started to become nervous. With Emily's left hand still in his, he knelt before her and pulled a ring out of his pocket. As he looked up into her eyes, they grew wide with surprise.

"Emily Middleton, since the first time I saw your picture, I knew that you were the most beautiful woman I'd ever seen. But after getting to know you, and seeing you grow here in Spruce Valley, I now know that beauty runs deep inside you as well," Josh said. "I see the way you treat other people, especially those children that you teach and the adults you tutor. I know things haven't been perfect since you arrived here, but I hope you'll agree to becoming my wife so that we can spend every day together for the rest of our lives."

Emily was so taken back by his unexpected proposal that at first she was simply speechless. But as he continued to wait on her response, she seemed to become alive with excitement as she began to nod her head.

"Yes, Josh. I'll gladly be your wife," Emily said with

enthusiasm. Josh smiled the biggest smile she'd ever seen as he slid the ring onto her finger and then stood to wrap his arms around her, being careful of her broken arm. He kissed the top of her head, but wanting more, Emily tilted her head up till their lips met. That kiss was filled with passion and desire but was so light that it was perfect for the moment. Josh broke the kiss, wanting to be respectful as he tilted back his head and simply smiled down at Emily.

"Well, I guess we better go tell the folks," Josh said. "I think they will be expecting the news."

"You told them that you were going to propose to me?" Emily asked as they walked hand in hand back to the inn.

"The other day I talked to them about it. And when I saw you walk into The Eatery tonight, I just knew I couldn't wait any longer," Josh explained.

"And what did your father say about it?" Emily asked, wondering if Mr. Ryder was going to lose his temper again once he saw the ring on her finger.

"He was happy to know that I was following my heart and proposing to the woman I'd fallen in love with," Josh answered with a kind smile on his lips. Emily stopped dead in her tracks, surprised to hear Josh's confession of love. She'd never really expected to fall in love before, but as she looked up into Josh's eyes, she felt like she could really love him in return.

"You love me?" she asked, searching his eyes for an honest answer.

"Yes, Emily, I do love you. That's why I asked you to marry me," Josh reassured her. "There is no other reason besides the fact that I do really love you." Emily's eyes filled with happy tears as she looked up at him. As best she could, Emily wrapped her good arm around his waist, wanting to hug him the best she could.

"Oh, Josh. I love you, too," Emily declared, thinking she'd never be happier in all her life. She couldn't believe that her heart could feel like this for anyone, but the more she thought of Josh's good character, she reasoned that there was no reason why she couldn't love this man for the rest of her life.

Josh hugged her back, tears filling his eyes. There had been a time when Josh was certain he'd never marry or have children. It had been a nagging fear at the back of his mind every time he found a decent minute to think about his future. He wanted to create a home with the woman he loved, and he felt such great relief in finally finding her.

Telling Josh's parents the good news was almost as exciting as experiencing the proposal itself. Emily was warmly hugged by Matilda and even Joshua gave her a decent smile. She felt reassured that when she married Josh that she would be joining a welcoming family that would honestly care about her. Though she knew that no family was perfect, she was at least happy that things could be mended before they were married. It was all so surreal to Emily as she simply felt pure happiness for the first time in her life.

CHAPTER 16

ear Emily, stop. I'm so happy for you, stop. I will send you a wedding present, stop. Cynthia, stop.

Emily held the telegram in her hands, a bright smile on her face. She'd stopped into Frost's to pick up a few items when he gave her the telegram. It was good to hear from her friend and she thought how kind it had been for Cynthia to take the time to send her a telegram from so far away. Emily knew that she would treasure it forever.

With it being Saturday, and the day before the wedding, Emily was making last minute preparations. She'd tried her hand at making decorations for the church and had just finished putting them up when she went to the mercantile to see if she could purchase any more white ribbon. She hoped to have the decorations done by this evening in order to enjoy a family-style dinner at the Slater's that evening. Josh told her that he'd pick her up at the inn, and therefore she had a bit of time left on her hands.

Emily went down the road to the women's seamstress shop, needing to fit into her gown one last time. Since the wedding had been rushed so that Mr. and Mrs. Ryder could return to their ranch, so had the wedding plans. Lucy had done her best to construct a wedding gown as fast as she could with also tending to a newborn, and now Emily had to try it on at the shop in case the other women needed to make any other adjustments. She was eager to finally try it on, and even more excited to be married tomorrow.

As Emily stepped into the shop, she was quickly greeted by Francene and Samuel. "Emily, you're getting married tomorrow!" Francene shouted with glee. "And I get to be your flower girl."

"That's right, my dear. I couldn't think of anyone else more perfect for the job," Emily said.

But Francene placed her little hands on her hips and said, "It's not a job. It's a duty." Emily chuckled as she watched the small child, thinking that it was very suitable and similar to the way she used to think about work.

"You're right, Francene. And how is Samuel today?" Emily asked as she turned her focus to the young boy who was often very shy.

"I'm excited for tomorrow," he replied in his soft voice.

"And so am I," Emily replied. Martha came out of the back room then and motioned for Emily to come on back. There, Emily spotted her wedding dress for the first time. Her mouth fell open as she looked at it, thinking it had much more detail than she ever thought would be possible for such short notice.

"It's gorgeous," Emily exclaimed, walking up to it on the

hanger and running her fingers over it. She'd never thought her dress would be made of silk because Spruce Valley was such a small town, but as she felt the fabric between her fingers, she could tell it was the real deal.

"Let's get you changed so we can see how well it fits," Martha said as she ushered Emily into the changing room. Once she was ready, Martha helped her into the dress while being mindful of her broken arm. It was the only thing that Emily wished was different. But she reasoned that she had to be lucky for even being able to be married to Josh. He was such a wonderful man and a well-looked-after gentleman in the community that she was simply honored to be marrying a man like him.

"My goodness, it fits like a glove!" Emily declared as she came out of the changing room and stood before the tall looking glass. "How on earth did Lucy do something like this in such a short time, and when she just gave birth?"

"That woman is a miracle worker for sure," Martha replied as she started to look over the gown. "I don't think I can spot one thing more to do to it."

"I would have to agree with you," Emily said as she turned around before the mirror to see it at all angles. "Well, I'll pay for this and get back to the church. I have some more decorations to finish up."

"Alright, let's get you settled then," Martha agreed as she helped Emily back into her day gown and then placed the wedding dress back on the hanger. "I'll wrap this up and bring it over to the inn for you."

"Just bring it with you when you come out to the dinner tonight at the ranch. I'm going to be spending the night there and coming in with the Slater's in the morning. Fiona promised to help me get ready," Emily explained.

"Sounds like we could turn it into a slumber party and have all the women sleep over," Martha suggested.

"My goodness, what a fun idea!" Emily said with a giggle as she came out of the changing room. "I think that would be excellent."

"It's settled then. We'll see you all tonight," Martha said as she began to wrap up the gown. Emily paid for the gown at the counter and bid the children goodbye before she left, feeling more excited than before. It had been a long time since she'd had a slumber party and wondered if any of them would get any sleep tonight!

"Are you sure you ladies are going to be okay on your own?" Sam asked as he stood by the front door, looking back at his wife and newborn as they sat in the sitting room. Lucy was rocking the baby to sleep, and he didn't like the idea of being away from them, even though he would just be sleeping in the bunkhouse tonight.

"Come on, Sam. Let the women have their fun," Gray said as he grabbed Sam by the arm and led him out of the ranch house. They'd just finished up having dinner together, and now the rest of the evening was left to the women.

"I'll see you bright and early in the morning," Josh said to Emily as he placed a kiss on her forehead.

"You bet I'll be there," Emily teased him as she hugged him one last time and finally let go. She watched as he left with his parents, needing to get them back to the inn. As the men departed, Emily turned to the women as they started to giggle with excitement.

"My goodness, what shall we do first?" Fiona asked.

"Well, it seems like mama and baby needs to get some sleep," Martha said, drawing everyone's attention to Lucy and little Maribel. They'd both fallen asleep in the rocker, and the other two older children had already gone off to bed.

"Alright, let's get them into a real bed," Emily agreed. The three women then carefully helped Lucy to her feet and led her to her bedroom before placing Maribel in the basinet, and helping Lucy into a nightgown.

"We're supposed to be helping Emily get ready," Lucy said as she yawned.

"I'm sure Emily is learning all sorts of life lessons by helping you two into bed," Martha said with a chuckle.

"Nothing truer than seeing a woman's body postpartum," Lucy said with a chuckle, causing the others to laugh. After Lucy was in bed, the other women returned to the dining room.

"How about a few rounds of cards?" Emily offered, thinking it had been a while since they had had a game.

"With the men out of the house, I think that's a grand idea," Fiona agreed. Martha quickly found the cards and toothpicks, and soon they were settled down at the table. Emily found the game very relaxing because it gave her mind something else to think about instead of the wedding tomorrow.

"Are you nervous at all?" Martha asked at one point.

"I wouldn't say nervous as much as eager," Emily

answered. "I don't know if I'll sleep a wink tonight because I'm so excited to get married tomorrow."

"Seems like you should start drinking if you're going to get tired enough to sleep tonight," Martha said with a wink.

"I'll go open a bottle of wine," Fiona said excitedly as she quickly got up from the table and disappeared into the kitchen. She came back carrying a bottle and a few cups. "The one thing I miss about Boston is drinking wine with dinner."

"You know, I didn't think about that until now," Emily said. "I feel there is much I've forgotten about my old life in Atlanta."

"But do you think that's a bad thing?" Fiona asked as she passed Emily a cup of wine.

"Compared to everything I've learned and gained by coming to Spruce Valley, I would say that it's a good thing that I've forgotten much about what it was like to live in Atlanta. I really had to change my way of thinking when I came here and it's all been for the better," Emily explained. Martha and Fiona were pleased to hear Emily say that. They, too, had really seen Emily transform into a better version of herself.

"I can tell that you and Josh are going to make each other very happy," Martha commented as she passed out cards for another round.

"I hope we will," Emily said with a sigh. "He's such a great person that I hope I can live up to that one day."

"Emily, you already do," Fiona was quick to assure. "In just a few months, you've moved to a new state, learned a new way of living, and even started teaching despite having never done it before. You have a lot to be proud of since you've gained such a good reputation in town." Emily smiled kindly at her friends, really appreciating their words.

"And based on the way that Josh looks at you, I'm sure you'll have a little one of your own before too long," Martha quipped, causing them all to laugh heartily. Emily was very thankful for her news friends. Though Cynthia would always hold a special place in her heart, she was grateful for having so many new friends who truly supported her.

EPILOGUE

*E*mily felt like she couldn't breathe as she stood at the doors of the church. They were currently closed, but inside she could hear the eager chatter of everyone who had come to attend the wedding. And since it was a small town and Josh was well known in the area, it seemed like everyone and their family had come to see Emily be married to Josh. Emily wasn't sure why she felt so nervous because she'd been in front of a crowd before, but reasoned that it had to be her excitement to finally be marrying Josh.

When the *Wedding March* began, Emily stiffened. But Mr. Ryder patted her good arm trying to help her calm down.

"Don't worry, Emily. You have nothing to be nervous about," Mr. Ryder said softly into her ear. Emily only nodded as she pushed a smile onto her face. The double doors were opened before her and though her eyes quickly scanned the crowd, they eventually settled on Josh. The moment their eyes locked, all the nerves left Emily's body. She was able to smile genuinely at Josh as Mr. Ryder led her forward. Everything else around her seemed to fall away as she only concentrated on Josh. He'd dressed in his finest suit and his light brown hair had been combed to the side and styled. She thought he was even more handsome than usual and was so happy to be marrying a man like him.

Josh couldn't believe how radiant Emily was. Her wedding gown made of silk seemed to glimmer in the morning sunlight that came in through the doors behind her. Josh saw her as a vision of an angel as she was escorted down the aisle towards him. He locked eyes with her bright blue ones and they seemed to twinkle as she smiled brightly at him, and he couldn't help but return the gesture.

By the time she'd finished being walked down the aisle by his father, something he was proud his father had agreed to do, Josh was eager to marry Emily and take her home to his apartment. But he knew that after the wedding, there would be a small reception at the Honeywell Inn. So many people had come out today to see the marriage that it wouldn't be right to skip out on the reception just to be alone with Emily. He'd have to be patient as much as he could.

Reverend Paul gave a sweet yet simple wedding ceremony. With it being Sunday, he tied a bit of his sermon into the ceremony, which neither Emily nor Josh minded. They smiled brightly at each other and made sure to recite their vows when the time came. Holding Josh's hands in hers made Emily fill up with such warmth and joy she'd never known before. Now, she wasn't sure why she'd been nervous before since it felt so right to be with him now.

As soon as the Reverend pronounced them man and wife,

Josh bent down and captured Emily's lips with his. It was an eager kiss filled with promises and want. It thrilled Emily no end, and when the crowd started to whistle, she broke the kiss and blushed deeply. She looked out over the crowd then, and took them all in for the first time.

She was happy to see all her students and their families had come out to see her be married. And she was even surprised to see Bright Star and a few of his tribe members attending as well. She recognized the Indian children that often attended school lessons and was happy beyond belief to feel their support today. Of course, Sam and Lucy were present with their two daughters, along with Martha and Fiona with their families. The women had stayed up late last night drinking and playing cards, laughing and carrying on, but by looking at all three of them, no one would have been able to tell. They were all excited for this day and all the joy it held.

Josh eventually led Emily down the aisle and out of the church. There, they thanked everyone for coming as the guests in the pews slowly made their way out. Those that were able to stay joined them at the inn for the reception where the joy of the day seemed to go on and on.

Nell had taken the time to prepare a special tea for Emily and Josh. Though Josh wasn't much into drinking tea, he could at least agree that Nell made the best he'd ever had. Emmet and Ella had been kind enough to cook a meal for the reception, which everyone thoroughly enjoyed. Even though Emily was still getting used to the local cuisine, she was finding that every new thing she tried she ended up falling in love with and was eager to learn the recipe for.

"What are you thinking about, Mrs. Ryder?" Josh asked

from beside her. For a moment, Emily thought that Josh was addressing his own mother, but then she remembered that she was Mrs. Ryder now, as well. She giggled as she looked at him, thinking herself rather silly in that moment.

"I think that I haven't been this happy in all of my life," Emily admitted. "I never thought that getting married could make me this joyful."

"I know how you feel," Josh said as he leaned forward and placed a kiss on her forehead. "I knew that I wanted to get married and start a family, but I had no idea how lucky I would be to marry a woman such as yourself. You've really proved yourself, Emily, and I couldn't be prouder." Emily's heart seemed to swell with even more love for Josh, which she didn't think was possible at that point. But it taught her that her heart was capable of growing larger than she'd ever imagined before.

At one point during the reception, someone pulled out a fiddle and began to play music. It had been ages since Emily had danced and though Josh wasn't eager to do so, he appeased his wife by joining her in the center of the room for a waltz. Emily quickly learned that dancing wasn't Josh's strong point, and together they laughed as Josh did his best not to step on Emily's toes. Her gown had been designed with such intricate lacework that he'd hate to have ruined any part of it.

"Let her dance with a real gentleman," Mr. Ryder said as he cut into the dance. Emily laughed as she watched the scowl that came across Josh's face, but it was soon replaced with a smile as he watched how elegantly his father danced with Emily.

"Never knew you could dance, Pa," Josh said as his father twirled Emily around as though he'd been born doing it.

"I'm sure I still have a few surprises up my sleeve," Joshua replied with a chuckle. Emily was pleasantly surprised herself to see that Mr. Ryder had dancing skills, and soon other couples joined them for a song or too.

Eventually the day gave way to night and everyone who'd come out to attend the wedding and reception eventually said their goodbyes. Matilda and Joshua said goodnight to the newlyweds and went up to their room while a few others stayed behind to help clean up the inn with Bill. With everyone departing, Josh knew that it was finally time to take his new bride home.

Arm in arm, Josh led Emily from the inn and over to the Sheriff's Office. There, he unlocked the door and pushed it open, revealing light within. Josh had purchased several new lanterns and planned to keep everything well-lit in case he or Emily were ever called away on important business. He figured that it would make the Sheriff's Office more welcoming and that the townspeople would be encouraged to stop in from time to time or come to him when they were in trouble.

"Looks a lot better in here," Emily commented as she looked around while Josh shut the door and locked it. "But I think it could use a woman's touch."

"Well, it's a good thing that a woman now lives here," Josh said as he then took Emily's hand and led her carefully up the stairs. "I not only added more light but also a railing."

"I can see that," Emily said as she let her right hand glide softly across the railing. She was looking forward to the day when she didn't need to wear the cast any longer and could write again. Writing notes on all her students' progress was difficult as it was. But as she stepped into the apartment with Josh, she was surprised once more by his kindness and thoughtfulness. The apartment had been decorated with new curtains, a few new furnishings, and a large rug that covered the center of the room.

"I know it's not as nice as the home you had back in Atlanta, but I wanted you to know that I do appreciate you and think you do deserve a nice place to live," Josh explained as Emily's eyes wandered all about.

"You know, Josh, I've come to learn that the best things in life are not things that I could ever buy at a store," Emily said as she turned to her husband. "And the best thing I've found so far is you." Josh and Emily embraced then, sharing a tender kiss as they both agreed that they'd finally found their true purpose in life.

The End

CAST OF CHARACTERS

- **Emily Middleton**
- **Josh Ryder**
- Dr. Sam Salter & Lucy Slater, children: Francene
- Sawyer Murtaugh
- Eddie and Fiona Murtaugh
- Bright Star, his sons are Running Bear and Sky Bird
- Gray & Martha Walters, children: Samuel
- Bill Eckert, owner of the Honeywell Inn
- Greta Royal, widow and housekeeper
- Mayor Delphina Stavros
- Elena, Delphina's daughter
- Reverend Paul & Annette Gibbons
- Drake, Sheep farmer for Dr. Sam Slater
- Robert, Drake's brother

- Mr. Frost & Mrs. Frost, owners of Frost's Mercantile
- Nell, waitress at the Eatery
- Zachariah Welliver, furniture maker
- Tom Barker, ranch hand

AMELIA'S OTHER BOOKS

Montana Westward Brides

 #0 The Rancher's Fiery Bride

 #1 The Reckless Doctor's Bride

 #2 The Rancher's Unexpected Pregnant Bride

 #3 The Lonesome Cowboy's Abducted Bride

 #4 The Sheriff's Stubborn Secretive Bride

Bear Creek Brides

 #1 The Rescued Bride's Savior

 #2 A Faithful Bride For The Wounded Sheriff

 #3 The Untangling of Two Hearts

 #4 Indian Bride for the Trusty Miner

CONNECT WITH AMELIA

Visit my website at **www.ameliarose.info** to view my other books and to sign up to my mailing list so that you are notified about my new releases and special offers.

ABOUT AMELIA ROSE

Amelia is a shameless romance addict with no intentions of ever kicking the habit. Growing up she dreamed of entertaining people and taking them on fantastical journeys with her acting abilities, until she came to the realization as a college sophomore that she had none to speak of. Another ten years would pass before she discovered a different means to accomplishing the same dream: writing stories of love and passion for addicts just like herself. Amelia has always loved romance stories and she tries to tie all the elements she likes about them into her writing.

Made in the USA
Monee, IL
15 September 2023

42788822R00118